HOLIDAY MUSINGS

By

The Lake Authors

Copyright © 2017 by
The Lake Authors

All rights reserved. No part of this book may be used or reproduced in any manner whatsoever without written permission except for limited use in classroom materials or in the case of brief quotations in critical articles and reviews.

Printed in the USA by
Create Space
A DBA of On-Demand Publishing, LLC

ISBN-13: 978-1973769095
ISBN-10: 1973769093

Acknowledgements

The Lake Authors is a group of published and serious writers who live in or near Lake of the Woods, Virginia. Our goal is to support one another in our writing efforts and to explore publishing opportunities as a shared endeavor.

This anthology is a collaborative project of the Lake Authors, and we thank everyone who contributed, edited, and assisted in its publication.

Special thanks go to Elaine Lewis for her art work, Julie Phend for coordinating the project, and Judy Hill and Jean Young for formatting and preparing for final publication. We are also grateful to our reading editors, Bronwen Chisolm, Mari K. Eder, Judy Hill, Allita Irby, Elaine Lewis, Julie Phend, Lois Powell, Carolyn Rowland, and Jean Young, and to Mari K. Eder for publicity.

We hope this anthology will surprise and delight you, and give you an idea of who we are and how we write. You can contact us at lakeauthors@gmail.com or follow us on Facebook at Virginia Lake Authors.

Original art for section dividers by Elaine Lewis

Cover Art Courtesy of Dan Reams, Photographer. Website: danreamsphotography.com

Holiday Musings
Table of Contents

SPRING		**1**
Early Spring Morning	Elaine Lewis	2
The Crock of Gold	C.A. Rowland	4
The Easter Bunny Did It!	Allita Irby	11
U.S.A.	Allita Irby	12
Hope	Elaine Lewis	13
SUMMER		**15**
Song of Summer Rain	Elaine Lewis	16
Miracles	Suzi Weinert	18
The Bride of Chucky Suite	jd young	28
FALL		**33**
Autumn's Call	Elaine Lewis	34
A Halloween Visitor	Julie Phend	35
The Gypsy's Secret	Bronwen Chisolm	41
That's Not My Job!	Chuck Hillig	73
Holidays Again	Madalin Bickel	77
A Thanksgiving Memory	Allita Irby	79
WINTER		**81**
Potomac Winter Leaving	Elaine Lewis	83
The History of a Holiday Fruitcake	Carolyn Rowland	84
Always a Fresh-cut Tree at Christmas	Allita Irby	93
The Christmas Chronicles	jd young	94
Home for the Holidays	Julie Phend	101
Third Grade Christmas, 1953	W. Rosser Wilson	109
A Christmas Story: Bensen's Letter to Grandma and Granddad	Mari K. Eder	112
A Colonial Farm Christmas	J. Allen Hill	118
Our Three-Hour Christmas Tour	Carol Zacheis	121
What Henrik the Elf Told Santa	Madalin Bickel	139
About the Authors		**155**

SPRING

Early Spring Morning
Elaine Lewis

Oaks at last
Let dead leaves loose
Kiting crisp cadavers
Onto bluster-brisk breezes
This time so often offers

Soon to bud
But naked still
Tall trees madly dance
To timeless tunes
Carried in the winds

Away still further
Backed by blue,
Rim-silvered clouds
Sail ever faster
Past my narrow view

Chased by winds
From distant places
These pristine shifting
Moisture sculptures
Bear scented tastes
Of far-off waters

Where bows of ships
On open seas were
Graced by wave and swell
Now all is carried here to me
With tales that only clouds can tell

Do these vast billows also bear
The sweat of fallen men - of
Warriors slain in foreign wars
Blood let and left on desert sands
To dry and rise as mist again

Or the sighs of tears
In far-off places
Sun-dried on faces
That I shall never see
Even so

I think I know
Those far-off waters
Tears and faces
Blood and men
And all are one with me.

The Crock of Gold
C.A. Rowland

Jack turned at the sound of the flapping paper.

His one-room thatched roof hut was tiny by most standards. Warm and cozy from the fireplace that burned year-round, wisps of smoke filled the air, tickling his nose. A hand-hewn wooden table with two matching chairs on one side served as a work area for his shoemaking business and a place to drink his favorite dandelion tea. A four-foot bed, just long enough so his feet didn't hang over, hugged the far wall.

But it was his prized possession which held a place of honor on the wide mantle above the fireplace that was his concern – his crock of gold.

"What the..." he yelled as he dropped the shoe he'd been working on.

In place of the round container normally filled to the brim with pieces of gold, a curled paper shimmered against the mantle.

He tore it off the hook and unfurled it.

NOTICE REGARDING CONTINUING LEPRECHAUN EDUCATION, he read. INCOMPLETE.

He slammed his foot to the ground. How could this be? He'd practiced before he'd gone to the required tests - disappearing in an instant, tricking a human so he could keep his gold and how to say one thing while meaning another.

He'd come home from the exam thinking he'd done fine. Now this.

He might have done more except they always seemed to tie the date to attend continuing education to the day before St. Patricks' Day. Meaning he should be out and about, drinking and celebrating with friends, instead of waiting for his results. Times like these made him wish his stamp had the power of Rumpelstiltskin's. Cracking the earth open would be fun. Instead, now his foot hurt as well as his back.

"Your crock of gold will be there when you know where to look," the paper read.

How stupid. If I knew where it was, then I wouldn't need to find it.

Why did he need CLE anyway? Being a leprechaun for fifty years should count for something. And the fairies all said his shoes were the best. His crock was always full of gold. Who were they to hide his gold anyway? Not passing your CLE meant the governing board could do just about anything until you passed.

He wasn't worried about passing – he'd manage that, but not having the gold was a real problem. How would he buy the leather to finish the shoes? Or the tiny nails or anything else he needed until he did pass.

Jack sighed. He'd have to play along with this and pass quickly.

So where to start? What part of the CLE had he not mastered that might give him a clue?

And why did they always have to hold the test in the human world?

He hated the very idea of it. Most people didn't believe, so he was always in danger of being stomped on as they hurried through their days. Or if they did see him, he had to scurry around to avoid having to grant wishes. He was much happier sitting at his bench making shoes. Why couldn't they let him be?

There was a new younger group in charge now. Thought they knew better.

Jack stared at the paper. He needed to go back to the testing area. Concentrating, he disappeared.

He reappeared on a dusty western street set. Hollywood and make-believe magic. Ironic and yet so appropriate. The set was still unoccupied. It had been modified so dummies dressed in period costumes stepped out from corners or shadows. Each had a paintball gun that shot red and yellow dye. The trick had been to anticipate where the paintball would be fired, disappear and then re-appear without being hit. Each leprechaun only had three disappearances to make it down the street. Duck and run was key with a few select vanishings.

Jack walked to the end of the street, searching for the yellow results listing. It fluttered in the wind, tacked to a tree next to the saloon. Jack moved closer. His name plus a black checkmark. He'd completed this task. This was not the lesson he still needed to accomplish.

Jack transported to the second site. It was a mountain, much like the one in the movie *Darby O'Gill and the Little People*. He'd seen the movie. Whoever had decided leprechauns had a king didn't know much about leprechauns. But the plot was okay.

For this challenge, Jack had allowed the human subject to name his three wishes.

He'd begun to wonder when the man asked for health.

"Success in work," the man said for his second wish.

"A crock of gold," he'd said with a smile. "That's my third wish.

Jack had known the man would ask for this. All humans did. It was only a matter of which wish.

"What about your fourth wish?" Jack had asked.

"I thought it was three wishes," the man said with a frown.

"I'm feeling generous today," Jack had said with a smile. "I've already given you the other things. One more is no more work."

The man had stared at him. Jack thought he might turn down the offer. But then the man reacted the same as in the film.

"Then I'll be generous too. Health for all my family," he said.

Jack had figured his acting must have rivaled Sean Connery. If the human in the test had seen the film, the man might have known there was a twist and Jack might not have passed this test.

"Is that your fourth wish?" he asked.

"Yes," said the man.

Jack had started to laugh and dance.

"Three wishes I must give thee,
and three were given one by one.
But you asked for a fourth,
and for that you have none."

It wasn't the same rhyme as in the movie, but Jack had thought it was quite clever at a moment's notice. The man's face had turned red and he stomped off.

Thinking about the scene again, Jack was sure he'd passed this test. He rooted around among the boulders until he found a paper tacked to a bush. Sure enough, his name was there with a black check mark. He'd passed. It had to be the last test.

Darn. He thought he'd nailed saying something but meaning something else.

His mind wandered back to the test. All of the leprechauns had been in a circle. The moderator said something to the first. There was a response Jack couldn't hear. Then the imp disappeared. Jack had been last. He'd thought the exercise was stupid and he didn't even remember what was said now. Only that he'd been left standing in the circle. Had the listing included his name with a black check mark? He'd been so glad it was over and so confident he'd passed each task that he'd wished himself home without checking any of the results. What if it wasn't there?

Jack whisked himself to the clearing. There wasn't anything around. Where would the paper be? The paper was always there – whether you passed or not. He needed to confirm what his mark was. He walked around. Where on earth did they put it? He found a rock and settled on it, seeing the clearing from a different point of view. It should be here. And then he knew. He could have kicked himself. The whole time, it had been about saying one thing but meaning another. Could he have passed? He didn't know. The fact that the paper wasn't there could mean he didn't. Or the lack of the paper was the clue.

Something clicked – it was staring him in the face. It was hiding in plain sight. It was the only answer. Jack disappeared and re-appeared in his hut.

He stared at the mantle and then the fireplace. He smiled. What led anyone to a pot of gold? He knew the answer – a rainbow. So where would you hide a cloud that could rain inside the hut? Jack pulled a chair over and looked up into the eaves, peering at each one. A tiny wisp peeked out.

Gotcha. Now all I need is a straw.

In the kitchen area, he jerked the cupboard open and dug through all the utensils. There it was – a fat blue straw. He grabbed his cup of water, crossed the room and climbed back up. He drew water into the straw and then breathed air and water into the wisp – the cloud expanded. Four times he drew and released until the cloud took shape and began to darken. That was enough. He could clean up a small puddle. Jack didn't want a flood on the dirt floor.

"Perfect," he said.

He climbed down and set the cup on the table.

Clap. He slapped his hands together. He waited, but nothing happened. Jack frowned. It needed to be the sound of thunder. Maybe he hadn't clapped loud enough. CLAP. He slammed his hands together so hard they turned red. He waited.

Crack! came the corresponding lightening. Then it rained. A light rain, but enough to cause the small rainbow hiding behind the paper to shimmer. At the end of the rainbow stood his crock of gold. Safe all along.

He just had to know where to look and to realize that the paper had said one thing, but meant another, concealing the answer.

The Crock of Gold was first published in the Kings River Life Magazine, March 30, 2013 issue.

The Easter Bunny Did It!
Allita Irby

Did you know that on Easter we get new clothes?

We get dressed up with patent leather shoes and hats and gloves
and then we go to church!

Did you know that the Easter bunny brings baskets of toys, and eggs, and candy?

That's why we have Easter so...
We can get new clothes,
We can get dressed up,
We can go to church,
AND the Easter bunny can bring us Easter baskets!

U.S.A.
Allita Irby

Around Memorial Day, folks get out their flags, red, white, and blue clothes and accoutrements. From Memorial Day through the Fourth of July, a sense of patriotism, nationalism prevails.

"My country good or bad, right or wrong!"

"The best country in the world!"

"These colors don't run!"

A family may have disagreements and fights within, but let an outsider say something about or do something to the family; that means war! The wagons are circled, the artillery comes out and bombs are dropped onto the enemy.

So pull out the tee shirts with bald eagles and old glory on them, the red, white, and blue buntings and the fireworks! Get out the grills, picnic baskets, hot dogs and hamburgers, watermelons and ice cream!

"United we stand and divided we fall!"

Hope
Elaine Lewis

Today I cannot tell you
How I remember days of sun
When we talked and laughed
As we trekked with all those
Small children through tall grasses
On the meadow's edge at Tahattawan
To hear birds singing and scary cows lowing
A real safari

My legs can still turn to jelly in remembering
How we'd collapse in laughter all the way home
From that mad, wild excursion
Into New York City where we found the Pope

How I think about the phone calls
"Good morning, star shine" or
"Stop the world, I want to get off"
Yes, there were days like that
How we could always share a tear
Or a poem or a thought

How our friendship had reached
Far beyond the shallows into
The murky depths of true feelings
Accepted unquestioned
Understood without explanation

How New Year's Eve has never been the same
Should auld acquaintance be forgot
and never brought to mind

The moments and the days and the years
. . . and the years
Will be remembered . . . and remembered

Today I cannot hold your hand and tell you
But I hold your heart in mine

SUMMER

Song of Summer Rain
Elaine Lewis

Ever peaceful, this porch-side scene
Of hemlock maple, oak and beech
Tulip-poplar, pine and birch
Laden in verdant shades of green
Is visited now with a summer rain

Soft-fall slip-drip spatters
Sounding on lush-leafed trees
Tattoo hidden patterns in
Muted whispered rhythms
Calling to an ancient core of me

Now the forest floor releases
Thinnest mists warm and rising
From yesteryears of leaf-life
In countless seasons sacrificed
The welcomed olden, molded scent
Of earth's summer thirsts quenched

Sights, sound and scents reach deep
To veil my vision like a gentle sleep
A sheer pale shawl that blankets all
Through which I am graced to see
Distant sights through delicate lace
That shift my present place in space

Mind roams on in unmeasured time
Far into centuries other than mine
Sensing olden soul connections

With every earthen living thing
And perceiving fervent persistence
In the ardent will of life *to be*

As in millennia before
And in millennia to come
The essence of a summer rain
Remains sufficient to sustain
A spirit journey still and deep
Like a solemn oath to keep

Whichever can inexorably speak
To that insistent longing
In our eternally lingering
Ancient core of being

Miracles
Suzi Weinert

If anything else went wrong today, this July 4th could be her worst day ever. Alison sighed and glanced at the clock: 6:30pm. Could she handle any more stress? She stared blankly at the to-do list in her hand.

She'd just hung up the phone, still absorbing the caterer's message. "Sorry, our truck's down, but we're working on it and we're coming. Just not at 6:30, as contracted. Set-up doesn't take long though, so don't worry. We'll be there as soon as we can. Okay?"

Not okay at all, but fussing at them wouldn't help. "Just remember," she pleaded, "thirty-seven hungry folks expect dinner tonight at 7:00pm."

Why wasn't this holiday easy like so many past ones? She remembered her childhood -- ogling dazzling firework displays, her exuberance at waving those once-a-year lighted sparklers as she raced her "torch" around her parent's yard. When her own children were little, they shared her excitement for this day's unique fun. Now they were all grown and married, with children of their own, but today, they'd gather here at home once more. Would this be her last July 4th with them?

Her neighbor, MaryAnn, talked her into the biopsy earlier this week. Alison hadn't told the family, not even Fred. Why upset her husband until she knew results? MaryAnn assured her, "As a nurse, I know the biopsy is a smart move." At Alison's dubious expression, she continued, "Relief if it's nothing or treatment if it's something. Win-win. And I can get you into the clinic fast because I work there."

Alison would learn the results in a few days, but the waiting felt unbearable with so much else on her mind today. And what if the results showed cancer? Had she inherited her mother's genetic vulnerability to this awful disease?

Her mother's birthday fell on July 4th and Alison again thought of this cherished person who died ten years earlier on this very day. What were the odds of dying on your birthday? Time scabbed the loss somewhat, but Alison missed her, unable to fully accept her death. How had her mother contracted lung cancer when she didn't smoke, nor did family around her? Alison grimaced, remembering those air-hungry gasps as her mother fought for breath at the end, when only pain meds eased her departure. Where was she now? Where did people really go when they died? "How about giving me a sign, Mom, that you're okay wherever you are?" Alison said aloud to the empty room.

She looked through the window into the back yard, where her husband, Fred, crouched by the pond on their wooded one-acre lot. In retirement, he'd become an amateur expert about this waterscape, its delicate ecosystem and marine residents. Each spring he added bullfrog tadpoles, a few baby turtles and water-cleansing hyacinth plants to join the twelve resident Japanese koi. Their distinctive coloring made each fish easy to identify -- he'd even named them. She knew that tossing a handful of koi food into the pond each evening drew these fish to the water's surface and a deeply satisfied smile to his lips.

Would Teresa come today? Alison's expression clouded at the thought of her thirty-year-old youngest daughter: an alcoholic. If so, what shape would she be in? Would her husband come with her? Were they even still together? Watching her child's life fall apart, Alison had suggested help, which Teresa ignored. What else might she do or say to bypass Teresa rebuffing her again?

Alison refocused attention on the list in her hand. Grabbing a pencil, she crossed off: delivery of rental tables/tablecloths, arrange chairs, set tables, fill water glasses, chill sodas and beer in metal tub, uncork wine bottles.

Back when she grew up, her parent's hospitality included open bar for guests in addition to generous food. She'd continued these gracious traditions in her own home. But now she wondered if easy alcohol availability had contributed to Teresa's addiction. If Teresa came today, would she head straight to the liquor cabinet? Had Alison unintentionally facilitated Teresa's destructive compulsion?

The doorbell rang as the first family members arrived. Her oldest son trouped in with his wife and three teenagers bringing along several school pals. After hugs and greetings, Alison asked, "Want to help Dad set up fireworks for later?"

"The tables look fabulous," someone remarked about the American flags and carnations in blue bottles and the red-white-and-blue confetti on yellow tablecloths. "It looks like the Ritz!"

On their heels came three more of her children with their families and more guests. Told the caterer would arrive late, they funneled out to the back yard. "Let's play bocce ball," one shouted. "No, let's swim first. Race you to the pool." Another added, "Maybe we'll see deer tonight. They live in these woods."

Alison looked past the familiar cars parked in front of the house, scanning up and down the road. No sign of Teresa's car. Nibbling her lip, she closed the front door in resignation.

Back in the kitchen, she looked again into the backyard, alive with people. Several of the men stood with Fred as he gestured toward his pond, other guests swam in the pool and some explored the adjacent woods. Several arranged fireworks to be lighted after dark, about 9:30pm.

She chatted with family members who drifted in and out through the back door for drinks or snacks she'd hastily concocted until the caterer arrived. But she glanced up sharply when the front door opened. Teresa! With her husband, right behind her.

"Teresa...Ed. How wonderful to see you both." Alison hugged them. "Everyone's here –

well, except the caterers. They're running late. How…how are you?" Would this cheeriness hide the concern she felt?

"We're okay, Mom. In fact, we're very okay. I didn't tell you sooner because I wasn't sure it would work, but I started rehab three months ago, and haven't had a drink since. I realized alcohol screwed up my life so I'm kicking it for good."

"Oh honey, what wonderful news." Alison felt relief, but shot an anxious glance toward the open wines at the bar, hoping they wouldn't tempt a relapse.

"Yes," Ed said, "she's determined to beat this. It's like a miracle in our lives."

Teresa hugged her mom. "And you played an important part, giving me the names of those rehabs and suggesting I try one. I finally listened." Tears appeared in Teresa's eyes. "Thank you, Mom, for believing in me even when I didn't deserve it." She turned to grab Ed's hand. "Come on, let's have a swim before dinner." Before they hustled outside toward the pool, Teresa looked back at her mother and blew a kiss.

Alison stared after her daughter until the ringing phone demanded her attention. "Hi, it's the caterer. We're a mile from your house."

Alison grinned into the phone, "Great. Come down the driveway to the garage. I'll meet you there. We'll put the buffet on the kitchen island."

Half an hour later, at 8pm, Alison stepped onto the back porch to ring the dinner bell. Cheers erupted as swimmers climbed out of the pool and the rest started inside. In the subsequent bustle of bodies, plates and food, they seated themselves and the meal began.

Midway through this holiday feast, Fred rose. "Thank you all for celebrating this holiday with us. Fireworks start at dark. You boys are in charge and can shoot them anywhere on our property except into my pond. Besides our family gathering together, today we also celebrate two birthdays: our country's in 1776 and Grammy's birthday. She's with us in spirit as we remember her today. Also, thanks to the caterers for this excellent spread," he nodded in their direction and everyone applauded. "And to your mom who planned the event, arranged the meal and bought the fireworks."

Everyone cheered and by the time they finished dessert an 8-year-old asked, "Hey, can we at least start the sparklers?" Fred nodded and the crowd moved outdoors while the caterers tidied the kitchen.

"Let's settle up now so I can join the others outside," Alison told the caterer. "Good job and thank you."

"Sorry again for being late. The leftovers are in your refrigerator."

When they departed, Alison started out the back door but stopped when the front doorbell chimed. She hurried to open the door, surprised to see MaryAnn.

"Bob and I are on our way to watch fireworks at his boss's house tonight, but I had to stop here first. When I took some papers by the clinic this afternoon, I happened to see your biopsy results. They'll call you soon, but I wanted you to know right away." Alison held her breath. "Benign!" MaryAnn chortled. They squealed with happiness, hugged and danced in a circle on the front porch. "Gotta go," MaryAnn said, "but I wanted to let you know right away." Alison waved as her friend hustled to her car.

In the back yard at last, Alison still smiled at this wonderful news as she handed out plastic jars to the grandchildren. "Do we get a prize for catching the most fireflies," one asked. "You bet," she confirmed.

Sparklers already twinkled around the darkening back yard as the grands danced about waving them. Alison stepped through the kids and adults to find her own sparkler, thinking, "If you don't light at least one on the 4th of July, you really missed the boat. Here's one for you on your birthday, Mom, wherever you are." The fusillade of tiny stars on her sparkler sputtered down the metal stick. When they ended, she doused the remains in a bucket of water Fred had provided.

The oldest son announced, "The lawn chairs are lined up. Anybody ready for fireworks?" At the answering cheer, he called out, "Okay, let the show begin."

Whistling fountain fireworks erupted on the ground, interspersed with fiery aerial bursts, blossoming into circles across the sky. During a re-lighting interlude, they heard scrambling in the woods before three terrified deer rocketed out of the woods toward them. Seeing deer grazing on the lawn wasn't unusual at dawn or dusk, but this was different. Alison jumped to her feet in alarm, as did several others. Panicked, the trio of frightened animals darted this way and that, terrified by the fireworks and thunderous sounds. One ran directly toward the line of lawn chairs, knocking Alison to the ground.

Struck in the lower chest, the blow knocked the wind out of her. She lay on the ground, unable to breathe and feeling dizzier as her oxygen ebbed. Fred and several others rushed to help, but their hovering forms vanished in the sudden light surrounding her. She saw her mother's smiling face, saying, "Alison, now you understand how hard it was for me to breathe and why I needed to let go. I am at peace, dear one."

Was this Alison's own death? The bright light and a loved one to lead her to the other side? This thought ceased abruptly as the light vanished, replaced by the summer night's darkness. She felt jerked to a sitting position and thumped on the back. The tightness in her chest eased and she gulped air.

"Let's go to the hospital, honey." Fred cradled her shoulders, acute concern on his face.

After several deep breaths returned her to normal, she shook her head. "No, I'm all right now. Just couldn't catch my breath, but I'm fine now. Let's finish the fireworks."

"Only a few more and then we'll start the finale, if you're okay, Mom," said one son. She assured him she was. "Then next come the bottle rockets," he crowed.

Six shimmering rockets erupted from their bottles and rose 30 feet into the air before descending harmlessly at a distance, but one bottle tipped left at the last minute, pointing the 7th rocket in an unanticipated direction. Mouths open, the crowd stared as the missile's arcing trajectory sped it inexorably toward the pond, where they heard the telltale splash. They stood frozen until Fred jumped to his feet shouting, "I said any place but my pond." He rushed to the water's edge, playing his flashlight beam across the surface to assess damage. Others gathered around him, craning to see if carnage floated atop the water, but saw only ebbing ripples. "That rocket's on the bottom," Fred gasped. "All those chemicals...my pond."

A hush fell over the group, the only sound a background of cicada drones from the dark trees. Nobody knew what to say about this flagrant violation of Fred's sacrosanct pond.

Then Teresa broke the silence, "As careful as the boys were, think how remote the probability that one rocket would hit the pond. What we've witnessed here is a miracle." She began to laugh and others did also, nervously at first. But, so contagious was this humorous relief that finally even Fred joined in.

Teresa whispered in her mother's ear, "Another miracle just like mine." Their arms encircled each other in the dark.

"Here comes the finale," shouted a son as he and his helpers ignited a fusillade of fireworks, filling the sky and yard with noise and lights. As this surreal display continued, Alison looked up at the sky. "Thanks, Mom," she whispered, "for your sign tonight. Love you, Mom."

She felt Fred's strong arm around her. "You all right, Sweetheart?"

"Yes, honey, I'm very all right. In fact, this turned into one of my best days ever."

The Bride of Chucky Suite
jd young

When our girls left home, Jerry and I moved to southern Virginia. Not a large home, but we now had two extra rooms. One became the TV/exercise spot, and I decorated the walls with Jerry's favorite car photos. The pull-out sofa in Jerry's room worked well if someone visited. My overnight company quota runs one or two visits per year.

The other had originally been destined for a guest room, but it made an exceptional second garage: stored furniture, craft items, holiday extras and pretty much anything that would not successfully thrive in the cold garage.

We now lived in a lakefront community and every Fourth of July, we're treated to fireworks set off from the banks of the clubhouse. We celebrate with neighbors in their boat and watch from a gorgeous lake view. Our daughter Samantha was anxious to visit and enjoy the fireworks and our planned barbeque festivities.

With Samantha's impending arrival, I started cleaning out and throwing away, but felt compelled to add some items – small dresser, desk, bureau – all *antique* garage sale items which I cleaned up and made attractive. Finishing with a couple of old mirrors, pictures of the girls' graduations, first steps, tiny scrawls of 'I love you mama' on pieces of paper – you know, the critical items a mother cannot let go.

A lovely new white trundle bed and patchwork comforter with a jillion throw pillows. The crowning touch was the girls' stuffed toys and dolls neatly arranged on the pillows. (Actually, most of their toys are packed in a super-sized vacuum space bag, but these few I could not squeeze out of my heart.)

It really did not matter to me that my *baby* had graduated college and worked on Wall Street. I thought she would love sleeping in the white trundle bed with the arched back, and the myriad stuffed toys, pictures of family members, little doilies on the table, and the baby mobile from her christening hanging in the corner.

Am I expecting too much? I mean – I like it.

I'm feeling really good about the *new* look of the alternative garage and couldn't wait to see Samantha's reaction. She came home, put down her bags, looked at the room and:

"Ma! What's with the room?"

"Do you like it? I was trying to…"

"Ma! It's freaky. It's a kid's room."

"Not really. It's our new guest room."

"You have my Cabbage Patch doll on the pillow!"

"I know. Did you notice I put your red velvet baby dress on her? Doesn't she look cute?"

"She? … Ma! … It's a doll … not a she! And you have my old Easter bunnies on the chair."

"MA! ... You have my mobile hanging in the corner. My mobile! You don't have kids anymore — why do you have a baby room? This is too weird."

Needless to say, I was crushed. Jerry stood at the door silently saying *I told you so,* which was fine – I would deal with him harshly at a later date. Let him wonder where the framed picture of his '57 Chevy went.

"Hey Dad, is Mama okay? Are you going to let people see that room? I can't have friends visit and stay in there. Has she seen a doctor or something? Is this some *empty*-nest thing? Really, is she all right? Can I do anything?"

"Mama is fine. Don't ask but she said something about wallpaper and, no, I don't know what kind. Just go along with her while you're home."

I set the table and prepared to start dinner. Samantha's friend Matt had arrived and I noticed him and Samantha chatting quietly in the corner. When I asked if all was okay, she replied, "Yeah, everything is fine. Matt just got a little freaked when he looked at the guest room and the Cabbage Patch doll was staring at him. He thinks it looks like something out of a Chucky movie – you know, like *The Bride of Chucky Suite*. He thought maybe you had adopted a kid or something. His mom threw all his old stuff out. Kind of a 'clean' look in his house."

I knew I had lost the battle and put the lasagna on the table, waiting quietly for dinner to end. Food was good – conversation was limited. Not nearly enough wine for my mood. And to think we were just starting the holiday weekend. Samantha decided she'd sleep on the pullout sofa in the exercise room.

I finished preparing the salads and munchies for our festivities planned for the next day, all the while wondering where I had gone wrong.

However, I would not think those thoughts when I sit with a lovely glass of brandy in the overstuffed, sage-green barrel chair with complimentary embroidered pillows, situated by the west-facing window with the lace curtains that allowed the setting sun to filter in on the flowered carpet and illuminate the stained-glass ornaments.

Life is good, and I wait patiently for the lovely fireworks on the lake.

FALL

AUTUMN'S CALL
Elaine Lewis

Still clinging fast to tall oak trees
Leaves spark brilliant burgundies
Until they fall - as must we all
And journey down
To leaf-strewn ground.

Now memories like falling leaves
Pattern pathways of my mind
Turning autumn's golden light
Onto visions - long-lost sights
Olden passions and delights

Sun-burst ruby flashes
Lay softest roseate touches
To those cherished cherub faces
All of whom have long since grown
Through life seasons of their own
And now are bravely bending
To the building and the mending
Of their own tomorrows.

Solace now is tasked by thoughts
Of all of those I've loved and lost
Those whose myriad intense energies
Still strive to be within the core of me
And strain my mind's eye to embrace
Each newly freshened familiar face
That I may know again and be with all
As I heed the dying glory call of fall.

A Halloween Visitor
Julie Phend

Halloween night — my first at Lake of the Woods.

I felt absurdly excited as I filled a bowl with mini-Hershey bars (my favorite) for the children who would be stopping by. When I was young, I loved trick-or-treating, and when I married, I looked forward to reliving that spooky excitement with my own kids.

But alas, that was not to be. My husband and I never had children and had always lived in an apartment in the city. City kids didn't go trick-or-treating, so I didn't even have the vicarious thrill of greeting them at the door.

Now it would be different. Single again, I moved to Lake of the Woods hoping to recapture the neighborly feel I had known as a child. The *Lake Currents* newspaper had specifically posted hours for trick-or-treating — turn on your porch light if you wished to participate.

So, by 5:00 p.m., my porch light was on, the treats in the bowl, and I was ready for visitors.

But none came. Not a single child on my doorstep, no packs of excited kids roaming the block. By 8:00, I had to admit they weren't going to come. Perhaps my house, tucked at the back of a small cul-de-sac bordered by the woods of Wilderness National Battlefield, was too remote.

I sighed and got up to turn off the porch light. Reaching for the switch, I peered hopefully out the narrow window beside the door one last time. To my surprise, I saw a lone figure walking up the pathway. A teenage boy — and in costume!

I felt a rush of affection for him — a kid who, like me, never outgrew his love of Halloween. I waited for him to reach the porch and then threw open the door, eager to hear him shout, "Trick or Treat."

He didn't say it, though — just looked at me with tired blue eyes. He was wearing some kind of old-fashioned military uniform, dusty blue with gold buttons up the front. There was a ragged tear in the sleeve, and his head was tied in a dirty bandage with what looked like dried blood leaching through.

"Nice costume," I said, holding out the bowl. "Trick or treat? You're my first one."

He frowned and shook his head. "No, ma'am," he said politely.

I looked past him for any little kids with him, but I didn't see any. "You're alone?" I asked.

He nodded, and the corners of his eyes drooped, making him look sad as well as tired.

I began to feel alarmed. Something must be wrong. "Can I help you?" I asked.

He nodded slowly, like he was considering my offer, and then said, "I can't find my friends. Have you seen them?"

I couldn't place his accent — it wasn't the Virginia twang I was getting used to, but not Midwest, either. Definitely not New York.

I shook my head. "I haven't seen anyone tonight. I thought there would be trick-or-treaters, but none came."

He sighed and turned to go.

"Wait!" I called on sudden impulse. "Won't you sit for a minute and tell me about it?" I pointed to the Adirondack chairs on the porch.

To my surprise, he nodded again. "Thank you, ma'am," he said. "I am right weary."

"Can I get you a glass of water?" I asked, but he shook his head.

He seemed skittish, and I didn't want him to disappear back into the night, so I didn't go inside for water, though I really thought he should drink some. Instead, I sat in the chair opposite him, enjoying the sound of the autumn breeze rustling the treetops.

"Your friends," I prompted. "When did you see them last?"

He shook his head. "I don't know. I've been looking for them a long while."

Indignation gripped me. If his friends were playing a trick on him, they had obviously taken it too far.

"Tell me what happened when they disappeared," I said. "Was it around here?"

"Oh, yes," he said. "These woods." He gestured vaguely to the woods behind my house. "Hard to see anything through these trees."

"That's the truth," I agreed. I'd already been lost more than once walking the trails back there. "Especially in the dark. But tell me everything you remember. It could help us locate them."

He scrunched up his forehead and scratched the back of his head. "Well," he said, "it was all so confusing. Jacob was by my side all day, as we tramped through that infernal wilderness." He shivered, though the night was pleasantly warm. "Seems like the trees rose right out of the ground to trip us up." He touched his bare head. "Lost my cap and tore my sleeve. Jacob slipped into a pool of slimy mud."

"You got off the path, then," I ventured.

He made no comment, just stared into the night like he was lost in memory. Then he shook himself and went on. "We couldn't find the others. We could hear them, though, all around us. But we didn't call out, not wanting to alert the enemy."

I blinked. Were they playing some kind of war game?

"And then darkness fell," he said, "and it was a hundred times worse."

Somewhere in the woods an owl hooted, and a cloud scudded across the moon. I shivered.

"It must have been scary to be out there in the dark," I said.

The boy nodded. "Hearing the mournful sound of that owl and the awful shrieks of the whippoorwill calling over the groans of the wounded. It was like they were mocking us." He fell silent.

Poor kid, I thought. He must be overly suggestible — reading all that Civil War history on the markers out there. And then being lost at night. It was enough to give anyone the creeps.

"But when did you lose Jacob?" I prodded, wanting to get him back to reality.

His eyes snapped shut, and a shudder went through his body. "I didn't hardly sleep at all, but I was comforted that Jacob was right there beside me. I felt certain we'd find the others in the morning."

I stared at him. Had he already spent a night in the woods? But before I could ask, he went on speaking.

"It was the longest night of my life. But then, just as the sky began to lighten, the whole woods broke out in a terrible racket. Muskets roaring, Rebels yelling, and the screams of men dying." He put his hands to his head as if to stop the noise.

"I looked over to Jacob to ask what we should do, and . . . he was gone." He shook his head and added, "I've been looking for him ever since."

He stood abruptly. "I should go," he said. "I must find Jacob."

He brushed past me, and I reached out to stop him. "Wait," I said. "We should call 911."

My fingers touched his hand, and I pulled back in shock. His hand was like ice.

When I looked up again, he was gone.

Vanished, into the swirling mists of Halloween night.

* * *

Author's Note:

Special thanks to my husband, Jack Phend, and the Friends of Wilderness Battlefield. Thanks also to Chris Mackowski, whose book, The Dark Close Wood, was the inspiration for my soldier ghost. The description of the Battle of the Wilderness in this story is based on the words of actual soldiers who fought in the Wilderness on May 5-6, 1864. The battle claimed the lives of 17,666 Union and 11,125 Confederate soldiers, many of whose bodies were never identified. Wilderness Battlefield land borders the community of Lake of the Woods, where residents sometimes see Civil War soldiers striding through their yards. When you walk in the woods of the Wilderness, you can still sense their mournful spirits.

The Gypsy's Secret
An All Hollow's Eve *Pride and Prejudice* Short Story
Bronwen Chisolm

Some passages are paraphrased from the works of Jane Austen

It was all Elizabeth Bennet could do to keep herself from skipping down the lane, but a proper English lady did not frolic. Regardless, there was an undisguised bounce in her step and she was unable to suppress the giggles, which escaped her lips from time to time. Upon reaching her home, she quickly removed her outerwear and rushed into the drawing room to share her news with her family.

Her mother jumped as the door opened and a hand flew to her chest. "Lizzy! You scared the life from me! What are you about rushing in like that?"

"Forgive me, Mama." Elizabeth dropped a kiss on her mother's cheek and smiled brightly. "I have news of the next assembly."

Her misbehaviour was immediately forgiven as her statement drew the full attention of her four sisters and their mother. Her eldest sister, Jane, still held her needlework forgotten in her lap. The younger sisters, Kitty and Lydia, abandoned the bonnet they had pulled to pieces and stood clutching each other's hands. Mary, the middle sister and most serious, laid her book aside, careful not to lose her place, and turned toward Elizabeth with a mildly curious expression. Mrs. Bennet grasped her second daughter's hands crying, "Do tell! Do tell!"

"As we discussed last evening, the full moon falls on October 31 this month, All Hallows' Eve. And since the harvest celebrations fall on the evening of a full moon, I suggested to the committee that we have a bonfire instead of the usual assembly. It was agreed upon, along with my suggestion that everyone dress in a manner outside their station." A spark of mischief shone in her eye.

Lydia squealed with delight. "Oh, shall we have hazelnuts to throw into the fire? I must know if Denny and I will be happy together."

"Yes," Elizabeth laughed. "And each household is to provide several turnip lanterns. Sir Lucas is seeing to the invitations and spreading the word."

"But what shall we wear?" Kitty asked in a whining manner.

"Well, Jane must wear her best dress, the white one. Mr. Bingley will surely be there and be pleased to see her looking so well." Mrs. Bennet smiled broadly at her eldest daughter. "She is already so beautiful; the light from the fire will give her an ethereal appearance."

Jane shook her head and spoke softly. "Mama, Lizzy said we must dress outside our station."

"Yes," Elizabeth quickly stepped to her sister's side, "but whether you are dressed as a milkmaid or the Queen of Sheba, you shall be resplendent, Jane."

"And what shall you wear, Lizzy?" Lydia asked.

Elizabeth shrugged her shoulders. "I am quite certain there is clothing in the trunks in the attic that will do."

Kitty frowned. "So it can be something old?"

"As long as it is not something you would be seen in normally."

Lydia began giggling. "Must it be women's clothing? Could we dress as men?"

A frown passed over Elizabeth's countenance. "We had not discussed that possibility." She thought a moment longer.

A loud sniff was heard and all turned their attention to Mary. "The church frowns upon such revelries. I shall not participate and I do not believe it proper for a *lady* to appear in men's clothing. The Bible forbids it."

"Oh, Mary, it is all in fun!" Mrs. Bennet turned away from her third daughter and smiled at her youngest. "Why would you wish to dress as a man, Lydia, when there are so many other ideas? We shall have the trunks brought down and see what can be found. Hill!" she cried for the housekeeper.

"Mama, please do not bother Mrs. Hill." Elizabeth moved toward the door to intercept the harried servant. "There is so much to be done with the harvest and preparing the turnip lanterns. I shall go into the attic and see what is there. Once I am finished, I will ask Mr. Hill to have the ones I select brought down."

Mrs. Hill stepped inside the room in time to hear, "Oh, very well. Never mind, Hill." She looked about confused, but quickly returned to her work.

Elizabeth grasped Jane's hand and pulled her to her feet. "Come, Jane, you must help me search."

"What about us?" Kitty asked, the whine still present. "You will take the best and leave us rags."

Jane shook her head. "Kitty, you know we would never do such a thing."

"*You* wouldn't." Kitty eyed Elizabeth suspiciously.

"Kitty, I promise we will not select our guises until everyone has seen what is there." Elizabeth quickly pulled Jane from the room before anyone else could protest.

"Lizzy, why are you rushing so?" Jane laughed as they tripped up the stairs.

Elizabeth lit a candle from the hallway lamp and opened the door leading to the attics. "I have no idea what we might find, and we may have to remake each of our outfits so we must decide quickly."

A giggle escaped her once more and Jane stood still, pulling her sister to a stop. "Elizabeth, what are you not saying?"

"Oh, Jane, I fear telling you for you will think poorly of me." A light blush covered her cheeks.

"I could never think ill of you, Lizzy. Whatever has you in such a state?"

Elizabeth's teeth rested upon her lower lip as she considered her response. "I suggested that we dress of a different station in order to see how Mr. Darcy and Mr. Bingley's sisters would appear."

"Lizzy!" Jane shook her head in disapproval, but a twitch at the corner of her lips revealed her amusement.

"They think so well of themselves, as though they are above us all. It is clear Miss Bingley has completely forgotten her brother is not a landed gentleman and her family's fortune was acquired from trade."

"And our uncles are in trade."

"Yes, but our father is a gentleman. She is not so much better than us though she was educated in a private seminary and has a respectable dowry."

Jane smiled as she brushed past her sister and began inspecting trunks. "Oh, beware, my Lizzy, of jealousy! It is the green-eyed monster which doth mock."

"Jane Louise Bennet, using Hamlet against me?" Elizabeth attempted to appear offended, but failed miserably and, with a laugh, opened the nearest trunk. "Perhaps I was not as courteous as I should have been, but I promise to do my best not to mock them at the bonfire."

"Lizzy, you know full well that given the opportunity, you will make sport of our neighbours and laugh at them in turn. It is what you and Papa do." Jane opened a trunk and began removing some of the contents.

A frown creased Elizabeth's features as she turned to study her sister. "It is not done to injure, Jane."

"I did not say it was." Jane pulled several wigs from the trunk and held them up for inspection. "Shall these do, do you think?"

Elizabeth stepped closer and examined the shabby hairpieces. "I suppose, once they are thoroughly cleaned, we might be able to do something with them." Her eyes fell to the remaining contents of the trunk. "Oh, look."

She reached down and took hold of a smaller trunk inside the larger. The lid was engraved with her initials, EOB, Elizabeth Ophelia Bennet. She tried the latch but it was locked and would not budge.

Jane leaned over her shoulder. "Perhaps is it our great grandmother's. You are her namesake."

"It well may be." Elizabeth ran her fingers over the engraving. "The workmanship is exquisite. Do you think anyone would mind if I put this in my room? I will look for the key later, once our disguises are decided."

Her sister had returned to searching the trunks and mumbled her agreement. Elizabeth set the box by the stairs and returned to their search. In a short time, they had determined which trunks should be taken below and manoeuvred them closer to the steps. Elizabeth took up the one containing her initials and carried it to her room while Jane went in search of Mr. Hill to have the other trunks moved to the back parlour where the sisters could search at their leisure without having to worry about making a mess. The back parlour had once been the mistress's study, but Mrs. Bennet disliked sitting away from everyone for fear she may miss some gossip or amusing titbit. Instead, the room was now used to store projects and materials that would otherwise clutter up the drawing room.

By the time Elizabeth joined her sisters, the first trunk was already open and its contents scattered about the room. Kitty and Lydia each had a wig sitting atop their heads and they were waving dusty fans about. Lizzy was surprised Kitty had not started coughing as her throat was easily irritated.

"You *have* had the wigs checked for bugs?" she asked, sending the younger girls into a tizzy. The wigs flew across the room as they each demanded the other inspect their hair. Elizabeth winked at Jane as she picked up the offending items and set them aside to be cleaned. She then turned to the clothing that had been tossed about and egan pairing up matching items.

"Oh," Jane cried as she leaned far into the trunk.

"What? What is it?" the younger girls asked as they rushed forward.

Elizabeth watched as Jane held out some hair pins with coloured paste beads while she placed her other hand behind her back. Their eyes met and Jane smiled causing Elizabeth to quickly turn away. Her angelic sister was hiding something from their younger siblings. Most uncharacteristic.

"Kitty, Lydia, why do you not take the wigs to Mrs. Hill and ask her to have them thoroughly brushed and cleaned. If it is done today, we may begin setting them this evening." Jane's explanation caused their protests to die off before they began and the younger girls left the room each holding a wig by their fingertips, as far from their persons as was possible.

"So what did you actually find?" Elizabeth asked when the girls were out of earshot.

"I believe I found the key," Jane replied as she extended her hand, the key lying in the centre of her palm.

Elizabeth took the small brass key and turned it over in her hand. It appeared about the right size. She was about to go upstairs to see if it would work, when Mary and their mother entered the room. She slipped the key into her pocket instead.

"Mary, I will hear no more on this subject. We will be attending the bonfire as a family. Mr. Bennet has even agreed to join us." Mrs. Bennet began looking over the items lying about. "Perhaps you could be a governess. You could carry a book with you since you always prefer to read. And look, here are your grandmother's spectacles!"

Elizabeth frowned, thinking Mary might well become a governess should none of them marry well prior to their father's passing. The family's estate, Longbourn, was entailed to a distant male cousin who could, if he so desired, turn the ladies out of their home upon his inheritance. If that occurred, they would be forced to fend for themselves as their uncles could not be expected to support them. Suddenly the idea of dressing outside one's station lost the appeal it once had. She excused herself and made her way to her room.

Sitting on her window seat, she stared out at the gardens and contemplated the bonfire. She had been so proud of herself for thinking of a way to pull the arrogant Mr. Darcy off his pedestal. Now she realized it would most likely make her family look even more ridiculous than was normal. A tear slid down her cheek and she swiped it away. She reached into her pocket for her handkerchief before more followed and was startled when she felt something hard and cold.

The key! Her melancholy blew away as quickly as it had come and she dropped down on the floor to pull the chest from under her bed where she had hidden it. The key fit in the lock but would not turn. Her brow drew together, wondering if it was the wrong key or if the lock simply needed oiling. She pressed a bit harder and the key moved a fraction, so she decided oil was the remedy.

She crept back downstairs, but need not have bothered being quiet as the cries and laughter coming from the back parlour would have covered any creaking of a lose step. After retrieving the oil from the butler's pantry, she returned to her room and allowed several drops to settle into the keyhole before attempting to turn the key once more. This time the key turned a bit easier. With a final forceful turn, the lock opened.

Elizabeth lifted the lid and looked inside. A sheer lace veil covered the contents and she carefully removed it. The stitches were so fine, she was reminded of the dew left on the grass in the mornings when she slipped away for her walk. She ran her fingers reverently over the delicate pattern before opening it to inspect it for damage. Though the colour had yellowed slightly in areas, there did not appear to be any snags or holes.

Catching a glimpse of herself in the mirror on the dressing table, she felt the desire to don the beautiful lace. She shook it out as she crossed the room and took a seat, then very carefully draped the veil over her hair. Once it was in place, Elizabeth found herself afraid to look upon her reflection. With a forced laugh, she shook off her nerves and raised her eyes.

The woman staring back at her from the mirror, from under the exquisite lace veil, was stunning. Elizabeth had never considered herself a great beauty, not beside Jane; but she knew she was not homely. In this one instance, however, she suddenly believed even Jane might pale beside her. Though the lace pattern was intricate, it was fine and did not obscure her features. Indeed, it seemed to cause her eyes and the colour of her hair to become more pronounced. Her mouth fell open and she continued several minutes in this posture until she heard footsteps on the stairs. The sound broke the spell and she quickly removed the veil, carefully folded it as she crossed the room, and returned it to the chest before a knock was heard at the door.

"Who is it?"

"Jane."

Elizabeth laughed. "You need not knock to enter your own room."

The door opened a few inches and Jane peeked inside. "I thought you may desire privacy."

"I did, but not from you. Come; see what I have found, but lock the door. I wish to keep this from Lydia and Kitty." Elizabeth opened the trunk as Jane closed the door.

"Oh!" Jane stepped forward, a hand reaching toward the veil. "It is beautiful."

"It is," Elizabeth whispered. "You must see it on."

Jane helped her to straighten the lace and stood behind her at the mirror. "You are lovely. Oh Lizzy, you must save this for your wedding day."

Elizabeth nodded, absentmindedly fingering the edges of the lace. "Do you think Great Grandmother wore it when she wed?"

"She must have." Jane moved toward the trunk. "What else did you find?"

As if coming out of a dream, Elizabeth removed the veil and joined her sister. "This was on top. I have not looked at the rest of the contents."

Jane took the lace and folded it while Elizabeth began removing items from the trunk. "It appears there are several jewellers' bags. I wonder what they contain."

She lifted out the first. The knot was tight, but with Jane's help they were able to open it. A chain and amulet fell into the palm of her hand. There were no gems, just strange etchings on the back. The front was polished gold with a fancy lover's knot engraved. Two hearts, one upside down and one right side up, twisted about each other forever entwined. She slipped the chain over her head; the pendant came to rest just above her cleavage, slightly hidden by her neckline.

While Elizabeth had been admiring the necklace, Jane pulled out the remaining pouches and lined them up for her sister to open them. Elizabeth glanced in the chest, and found bundles of herbs tied with ribbons. Each bundle appeared to be a different mixture and each ribbon had been dyed a different colour. The leaves were frail with age and the cloth faded, so she decided it best to leave them lay.

Instead, she reached for the next pouch. It was the smallest of the velvet pouches and she suspected it held a ring. When the contents fell into her palm, her suspicions were confirmed, but it was a man's ring. She held it up, finding a similar Celtic design engraved into the gold. The ring was returned to the pouch and placed gently upon the herbs, sending up a weak scent of yarrow.

Elizabeth smiled at her sister and reached for the next pouch. A series of chains connected to a small ring dropped into her hand. She held it up, twisting it from side to side, but was unsure how it was to be worn. She attempted to slip the ring on a finger, but it did not pass the first knuckle on any but the smallest.

The chains fell over the back of her hand, wrapping about her wrist and Jane cried out. "Oh, I know what that is. Lizzy, do you not remember the pictures of the gypsies we found in Papa's study when we were little? One of them wore a ring on her toe with chains going up the foot that wrapped about the ankle."

Elizabeth did remember and she studied the item closer. "Why would Great Grandmother have a piece of gypsy jewellery?"

With a shrug of her shoulder, Jane leaned closer for a better look. As she did, she knocked the chest and the herbs shifted releasing a mixture of patchouli, yarrow, and lavender. "I am surprised the scents are so strong. I would have thought they would be completely dried out by now." She placed a hand to her head. "What do you think Mr. Bingley will wear to the ball?"

"I am sure I do not know." Elizabeth replied distractedly. She returned the strange piece to its pouch and then to the chest, along with the pouch from the amulet. Closing the lid, she relocked it and slid it under her bed. The key she slipped into her pocket.

"Shall we return to see what Lydia and Kitty have chosen to wear?"

With a nod, Elizabeth followed her sister from the room. For the rest of the evening she found her hand continually brushing against her skirt, reassuring herself of the presence of the key.

* * *

The day of the All Hallows' Eve bonfire and ball arrived and spirits were high at Longbourn. Each of the sisters were pleased with their guise, though it had been decided the others would have to guess what they were.

Following her mother's suggestion, Mary had indeed chosen to appear as a governess. She had found an old dress that was near ready to be given to the poor and dyed it black. Surprisingly, the dark dye gave a lustre which brought new life to the otherwise drab garment. The spectacles hung from a chain about her neck as they hurt her eyes to actually wear them. She sat upon the drawing room sofa, her books in her lap as she waited for her sisters.

Kitty had chosen to dress as a French modiste. She adopted a French accent and wore an apron with many pockets. Each held a number of tools including pins, scissors, buttons, a spool of thread, a piece of paper, and a pencil. She also carried the latest French catalogue received from her Aunt Gardiner in London.

She entered the room closely followed by Lydia. The youngest Bennet sister had not been able to convince her father to allow her to dress as a man. Much to that man's dismay, she settled for a barmaid instead. With her cleavage displayed to advantage and a swath of cloth wrapped about her hips like an apron, she carried a mug in one hand and a pitcher in the other. Her mother was pleased to see both items were either cracked or chipped and would not be missed should her daughter set them down and forget to retrieve them.

Jane entered next to her mother's exclamations. It had been quite difficult for her to decide upon a guise, but in the end Elizabeth had helped. Finding the oldest gown in the attic and raiding the basket of baubles, they had constructed a costume worthy of any Shakespearean stage. The freshly styled and powdered wig along with a strand of paste beads finished her ensemble beautifully.

"Have I the pleasure of Lady Macbeth or Katherina?" Mr. Bennet asked as he bowed over her hand.

Elizabeth laughed. "Who could think our sweet Jane capable of either role? I believe Bianca would be the better choice."

All eyes turned to her and silence descended. Mrs. Bennet's gasp broke the spell, quickly followed by Lydia and Kitty's cries.

"I knew she would save the best for herself!"

"Where did you find that?"

"Lizzy, whatever are you wearing?" her mother demanded.

A blush crept over Elizabeth's features as she glanced down at her clothing. "I found Great Grandmother's trunk. It has my initials on it. This ankle jewellery was inside and it reminded me of the gypsy pictures in Papa's study. I simply layered several skirts, pulling some up here and there to reveal the others beneath."

Her father started at the reference and he knelt before her to examine the ring and chains upon her foot. "Is this the first you have put it on?"

She nodded, confused by the question.

"You cannot allow her to go to the ball in her bare feet!" Mrs. Bennet exclaimed.

Mr. Bennet frowned as he stood and looked her over. "I see nothing wrong with her guise. It is no more revealing than Lydia's."

"I care not how low the neckline plunges, I am speaking of her ankles and her bare feet." Mrs. Bennet stepped closer to her daughter and grasped the pendent about her neck. "What is this? I have never seen it before."

"I suspect she found it in the trunk as well as it belonged to my grandmother." Mr. Bennet sighed and began ushering his family into the hallway.

Mrs. Bennet appeared quite upset, though Elizabeth was uncertain why. She had been particularly careful in her choices, not wishing to embarrass herself or her family. She had even packed a small bag with stockings and slippers she intended to wear once the dancing began.

Her father directed everyone into the carriage before mounting his horse and following along beside. From her seat, Elizabeth could see him and realized he was deep in thought. From time to time, he would glance in her direction and frown. For the first time in her life, she felt his displeasure.

The carriage stopped in a side street at Meryton, near the square where the bonfire had been built. The sun had not yet set, and individuals were making their way toward the area carrying stray bits of wood and turnip lanterns.

Mr. Bennet dismounted and began handing his ladies out of the carriage. Elizabeth was last and he placed her hand upon his arm before turning to make their way toward the festivities.

"Papa," she said softly.

"Yes, my Lizzy."

"Have I done something to displease you?" Tears filled her eyes and she bit her lip, hoping to keep herself from crying.

Mr. Bennet took a deep breath and released it slowly. "No, child, but I fear you set yourself on a path you may not have chosen knowingly."

She looked at him, waiting for some explanation, but he said no more. Elizabeth was just about to ask what he meant when they encountered Sir William Lucas and his family a block from the square.

"Well, well," Sir William cried after greetings were done. "The Bennet family will surely be the talk of the ball."

In her current state of mind, Elizabeth was unable to determine if this was meant as a compliment or censure. Her knowledge of the gentleman would normally have assured her of his goodwill. Tonight, it simply added another question.

"Eliza." Charlotte Lucas took her hand. "How daring, a gypsy!"

Forcing a smile, she looked her dearest friend over. "And you, Charlotte, a pirate?" A younger Lucas' toy sword strapped at her hip, and perhaps the oversized boots, were the only things that distinguished Charlotte's guise from any other.

The ladies moved forward, leading their families toward the gathering crowd. "I was surprised by the theme for this evening's assembly. Do you think many of our neighbours will decline to attend?"

Elizabeth glanced about at the number of people, most dressed in some guise. "It does not appear that will be the case."

"And what of the Netherfield party? Papa said Mr. Bingley was pleased with the idea, but I wonder if the others will be."

A warmth covered Elizabeth's countenance. She had forgotten Mr. Darcy and the Bingley sisters. What would *they* say of her appearance? Taking a deep breath, she pushed her doubts and fears from her mind in an attempt to reclaim the excitement that had filled her as she dressed. She was determined to enjoy the evening.

They rounded the last corner and found the square quite full. Several soldiers stood about in groups with young ladies nearby. Each sported their normal red coats and Elizabeth wondered if it were due to lack of resources or their Colonel's orders. As she did not see a single officer out of uniform, she decided it was the latter.

"Miss Elizabeth. Miss Lucas."

They turned to find Mr. Denny approaching from Elizabeth's left and waited until he was beside them. "Good evening, Mr. Denny," Elizabeth greeted him as she curtseyed. "I am sorry to see the militia was unable to join in the fun of dressing outside one's rank."

He bowed before giving her a dimpled grin. "I believe Colonel Forster feared we would overreach."

"Ah, but if you look about it is clear most chose to dress below their station." Charlotte waved her hand toward the gathering and Elizabeth saw she was correct.

"But not all have arrived," Mr. Denny added with a wink. "May I secure a dance with each of you before your cards are full? I have already been promised the first and second by the youngest Miss Bennets."

"Well then, sir, you may claim me for the third." Elizabeth felt her spirits rise as her thoughts turned to the dancing.

"I would be pleased to dance the fourth with you, sir," Charlotte replied.

"Capital! If you will excuse me, Miss Lydia appears to require my presence." He bowed and moved past them.

Elizabeth glanced about in time to see her youngest sister waving frantically to the officer. She shook her head, but was glad to see Jane moving toward Lydia. Hopefully she would be able to curb their sister's enthusiasm.

"Look, Eliza! The Netherfield party has arrived." Charlotte tugged her arm discreetly and nodded toward the far side of the square.

Just on the other side of the bonfire site, Elizabeth was able to make out four individuals. Miss Bingley was the first to be seen as her headdress stood higher than her brother's head. The siblings were close in height, though he normally topped her by a few inches. Tonight he could not be seen had he stood behind her. The turban itself was large, but the feathers pinned to it gave it even greater height. Elizabeth wondered what, other than a sign of wealth, it was meant to be. From where she stood, the remainder of Miss Bingley's clothing was concealed from view.

Mr. Bingley wore an unusual outfit which Elizabeth recognized as an Indian kurta and pants. Her uncle had travelled to India once on business and returned with such an outfit. He had expressed his pleasure in wearing the clothing; finding it far less restricting than a proper jacket and pantaloons, though not warm enough for the London winters.

Mr. and Mrs. Hurst did not appear to be in disguise at all. Their clothing appeared quite similar to what Elizabeth had seen them wear during her time at Netherfield. It was as she had suspected, they would not lower themselves to such a display. She anxiously looked about to see what the great Mr. Darcy had chosen to wear, but did not see him. She was surprised by her disappointment when she considered that he had chosen not to attend.

"Well, Lizzy, are you happy?" Jane's soft voice seemed to echo her conscience's tease. "Mr. Bingley and his party have attended and dressed accordingly."

Elizabeth looked to her sister, clearly puzzled. "I see that Mr. Bingley has indeed embraced the spirit of the theme, but not his sisters or brother."

"What could you mean? Miss Bingley appears as though she is about to perform an aria for the prince regent himself and the Hursts are clearly a housekeeper and butler."

Elizabeth looked again and realized her sister was indeed correct. The party had moved nearer and Miss Bingley's dress and jewellery did appear as though it belonged upon a stage. The Hursts had now removed their outerwear and revealed their guises. Mrs. Hurst wore an apron and bonnet while Mr. Hurst was indeed in a butler's uniform. Elizabeth wondered where he had obtained it as she knew of no butlers in the area who matched the gentleman's girth.

The party began making their way toward the older Bennet sisters, but Elizabeth still had not seen Mr. Darcy. Before they were near enough to hear, she commented on it to Jane.

"Perhaps they were separated."

"Perhaps he decided he was above such a display."

Jane was unable to reply as Mr. Bingley stepped before them at that moment, but she looked sadly upon her sister. Elizabeth blushed, knowing she had disappointed her dear sister.

"Miss Eliza, how very shocking." Miss Bingley feigned dismay over Elizabeth's guise. "A gypsy?"

"And you, Miss Bingley, an opera singer?" She forced a smile. "Shall you perform for us this evening?"

"If you will dance. Have you brought your finger cymbals?"

"Alas, I left them home this evening."

"What a shame."

"Indeed." A deep voice sounded behind her, causing Elizabeth to startle.

She turned to find Mr. Darcy wearing a simple shirt and worn buckskin trousers. He looked as though he had just come from mucking out the stables.

"Mr. Darcy." She curtseyed. "I am surprised Netherfield boasts a stable boy of your stature." The words tumbled from her lips before she had the opportunity to stop them.

"They are my own, Miss Elizabeth."

Her eyes widened in surprise. "Truly?"

Amusement danced across his countenance. "Truly. There are times even a gentleman finds the need or desire to exert himself in a manner impinged upon by his normal wardrobe." His eyes drifted down over her clothing, resting a moment on her bare feet, before returning to her now blushing countenance. "And your guise? Is it your own?"

"Items found in our attic, sir." She looked away.

"You have gypsy blood, Miss Elizabeth?"

She turned to meet his gaze once more, expecting to see disgust, but found herself drawn to him instead. "None of which I am aware. I know not how my great grandmother came to possess such items."

The sun began to set and the notes of the musicians tuning their instruments filled the air. Mr. Darcy bowed to her once more.

"May I request a dance, Miss Elizabeth? Have you the ... second available?"

Before she could reconsider, Elizabeth agreed.

The little group began making its way closer to the site of the bonfire. Mr. Bingley escorted Jane on his arm with the Hursts close behind. Miss Bingley claimed Mr. Darcy's arm, though the gentleman glanced toward Elizabeth.

She linked arms with Charlotte and set a pace to discourage any further conversation.

Charlotte laughed softly as they neared the assembly. "It appears your guise has attracted Mr. Darcy's attentions."

"Do not be silly, Charlotte. He was simply being polite."

"He was not polite to Miss Bingley, Mrs. Hurst, or myself."

"Perhaps he has already secured dances with Miss Bingley and Mrs. Hurst." Elizabeth frowned.

"Then I feel doubly insulted to be so overlooked."

Elizabeth looked to her friend but saw immediately Charlotte was in jest. "Nothing will come of it."

Her friend would only respond with an amused grin.

In short time, the bonfire was lit and the music began. Elizabeth stepped to the side to remove the chains about her ankle in order to don her stockings and slippers, but was unable to open the clasp. She motioned for Charlotte to assist her, but she too found herself not up to the task.

"Miss Elizabeth, is there a problem?" Mr. Darcy asked as he approached.

Elizabeth bit her lip as she debated telling him of her dilemma. Not knowing what else to say, she explained that the clasp would not open.

"May I?" he asked as he knelt before her.

With heat surging across her cheeks, she slowly nodded. A moment later, the chains fell from her foot.

"Thank you, sir," she said with relief. She had been fearful she would have to sit out of the dancing or, worse, dance barefoot and risk having her toes trod upon.

"This is a surprise." Mr. Bennet stepped from the nearby shadows and approached the small group. "Well, what have you to say for yourself, Mr. Darcy?"

The gentleman looked confused, glancing between Elizabeth, Charlotte and Mr. Bennet. "Pardon me, sir, but I do not understand your meaning."

"The chain you hold in your hand is a family heirloom. It can only be removed by the lady's intended."

Elizabeth gasped.

"Intended?" Mr. Darcy asked.

"Yes. Elizabeth did not know when she wore it this evening. Had I known she had found it, I would have warned her." Mr. Bennet reached out and took the jewellery from Mr. Darcy's open palm. "My great grandfather had promised my grandmother to a gentleman. He was rumoured to be a vicious man, but wealthy and with excellent connections. Her mother, knowing her daughter would never be happy with such a man, consulted the gypsies and obtained three items. They instructed her to have her daughter wear this amulet." He pointed toward the pendant about Elizabeth's neck. "It would draw the gentleman of her choice to her. She was then to wear this." He held up the chains and toe ring. "For only the man who truly loved her would be able to remove it."

There was silence for a moment before Darcy's hoarse voice said, "And the third?"

"A man's wedding band."

"The one I found in the trunk with these other items," Elizabeth whispered.

Mr. Bennet nodded. "So, I ask again, what have you to say for yourself?"

Mr. Darcy swallowed hard, his gaze moving rapidly between Elizabeth and her father. "Is this a trap? Are you accusing me of compromising Miss Elizabeth?"

Shaking his head, Mr. Bennet sighed. "No. Miss Lucas has been at Elizabeth's side all evening. She even attempted to remove the chains, but was unable."

Elizabeth felt the fear rising within her. "But that signifies nothing, Papa. I am certain anyone could have removed the chain. Mr. Darcy was simply the first to attempt it besides Charlotte and myself."

Mr. Bennet nodded slowly. "Very well." He knelt before her and replaced the ring and chains. Standing, he took her hand and led her toward a small group of officers with Charlotte and Mr. Darcy following closely. "Gentlemen, we have a dilemma. My daughter is unable to remove her foot jewellery and requires assistance."

Each of the officers knelt before Elizabeth, one at a time, and attempted to remove the chains, but were unsuccessful. Mr. Bennet then led her toward Mr. Bingley and his party. Again, the chains could not be removed.

"Shall we continue?" he asked Elizabeth and Mr. Darcy.

The couple looked to each other, but said nothing.

"Very well," Mr. Bennet sighed and called additional men and women over to attempt to remove the chains. All failed.

"Mr. Darcy, will you assist my daughter?"

Elizabeth felt her heart race as the gentleman once more knelt before her. Reverently, he reached out, opened the clasp, and the chains fell away from her ankle. A cheer went up from the crowd and they disbursed, returning to the festivities. Neither Elizabeth nor Mr. Darcy moved. They were unable to meet the other's gaze. Tears slid slowly down Elizabeth's cheeks.

She could not deny she found Mr. Darcy attractive. Elizabeth would have laughed and forgotten his slight at the September assembly if she had not felt drawn to him the moment she saw him. Additional conversations had shown him to be an intelligent, if arrogant, man. He was someone she would have respected had he treated those around him differently.

"Papa?" Her voice was a hoarse whisper. "What happened to Great Grandmother? Did she marry the man her father chose or the man who removed the chains? Was she happy?"

Mr. Bennet cleared his throat, his eyes settled on Mr. Darcy who remained on the ground before Elizabeth, the chains cradled in his hands. "You would be surprised to find the man who removed the chains was the man her father had chosen. And yes, they were one of the happiest couples I know."

Elizabeth gasped. "But you said he was a vicious man."

"I said he was *rumoured* to be a vicious man. Sometimes things are not as they appear." He turned toward Charlotte. "Miss Lucas, would you like some refreshment?" He offered her his arm which she accepted, and escorted her away from the silent couple.

The moment they were alone, Mr. Darcy began to speak. His voice was soft and full of emotion. "Elizabeth ..."

"Please, Mr. Darcy, there is no need ..." Elizabeth turned to move away, but he reached out and caught her hand.

"Perhaps not, but ... I must ... You cannot imagine ..."

The frustration written on his features was nearly comical, but Elizabeth could not laugh. She stared at him, uncertain of what he was attempting miserably to say.

Mr. Darcy closed his eyes and took a deep steadying breath before rising and standing before her. He still maintained possession of her hand, which he cradled in both of his. The gypsy chains rested between their palms. When he spoke, his voice was steadier.

"In vain have I struggled. It will not do. My feelings will not be repressed. You must allow me to tell you how ardently I admire and love you."

Elizabeth's breath caught in her throat. She attempted to draw her hand from his, but he clasped it tighter. Before he could continue, she raised her eyes to his in challenge. "How dare you say such things? It has been but a month since you declared me tolerable but not handsome enough to tempt you. You now say you admire and *love* me?"

As she spoke, Mr. Darcy's colour rose. When she stopped, he was no longer able to hold her gaze. His eyes fell to their joined hands and he caressed the back of hers. "My behaviour that evening was unacceptable. Please accept my apology for my rudeness. I ... I have not the talent which some people possess of conversing easily with those I have never seen before. I cannot catch their tone of conversation, or appear interested in their concerns, as I often see done." He swallowed and looked once more into her eyes. "Perhaps I should have judged better, had I sought an introduction, but I am ill qualified to recommend myself to strangers."

The anger surging through her at his initial declaration ebbed as she witnessed the vulnerability in his gaze. "You are a man of sense and education, who has lived in the world, yet you declare yourself ill qualified to recommend yourself to strangers? So you would separate yourself instead? Walking about the room, speaking only to your own party? Showing your disdain for those not of your status?"

"Disdain? No. Elizabeth ..."

She could not stop herself from flinching as he used her Christian name. Her response shocked her, after all, how often did he call her *Miss* Elizabeth. Perhaps it was the way it slipped off his tongue as though caressed. Or his hands still holding her own in such a familiar manner. She glanced about, but it appeared no one was near.

"I may be a selfish being in practice, though not in principle. As a child I was taught what was *right*, but I was not taught to correct my temper. I was given good principles, but left to follow them in pride and conceit. Unfortunately an only son (for many years an only *child*) I was spoiled by my parents, who though good themselves (my father, particularly, all that was benevolent and amiable), allowed, encouraged, almost taught me to be selfish and overbearing, to care for none beyond my own family circle, to think meanly of all the rest of the world, to *wish* at least to think meanly of their sense and worth compared with my own."

Elizabeth stared at him, attempting to reconcile what he said with the few facts she knew of him. In truth, he had not spoken to the people of Meryton more than necessary at the assembly, but she had seen him conversing with Colonel Forster at Lucas Lodge as well as a few of the other gentlemen. Overlooking his insult, he had spoken to *her* respectfully and in a somewhat friendly manner. Though he spoke now of pride and thinking meanly of those beyond his family circle, his friend was a descendent of trade yet he offered his assistance freely. She shook her head and looked about once more until her eyes fell on a nearby bench.

"May we sit?" she asked.

He nodded, placed her hand upon his arm, and escorted her to the bench she indicated. She immediately noticed the loss of his warmth. They sat close, but not touching. Mr. Darcy absent-mindedly fiddled with the delicate chains, slipping the ring on the very tip of his smallest finger.

"Careful." Elizabeth could not keep the amusement from her voice. "You do not wish to be trapped in that."

His eyes fell to his hands before he met her gaze and saw the humour there. A smile broke across his countenance and stole her breath. She shook her head once more in amazement as her mind returned to her previous thoughts. What did she truly know of this man before her?

"You appear so serious." There was a vulnerability in his voice that she had not heard before.

"I am attempting to illustrate your character."

"And what is your success?"

She shook her head. "I do not get on at all. You present such different accounts as puzzle me exceedingly."

"I?"

"Yes, you appear to think meanly of the world and say that you were raised in such a manner, yet you befriend Mr. Bingley. He is not of your circle, I am certain."

Mr. Darcy frowned. "No, he was not born a gentleman, but he is all that is amiable. I could not ask for a more devoted friend."

"You protect him, I think."

Mr. Darcy nodded. "He is too trusting."

Elizabeth mimicked his posture and actions. "As is my sister."

"Elizabeth, it is clear you know little of me. This evening, your father's revelation, my hasty words; they must be overwhelming. Shall we begin again? May I call upon you?"

Suddenly the sounds of the musicians and the revelry broke through the spell that had weaved about them. Elizabeth gazed into his eyes and nodded.

"I believe this is our dance, sir."

That's Not My Job!
Chuck Hillig

Once it was determined that Jimmy was to be the "A-Hole-of-the-Night," the rest of us proceeded to get righteously drunk. No, ole Jimbo wasn't an A-Hole in the usual sense of the word. It was just that it was his sorry lot to have been chosen as the designated driver for the "Gang-of-Four" that night, and so the A-Hole part of it just went along with the job. After all, as the elected Big Daddy (read "scold"), he was responsible for stopping the rest of us from any craziness being fueled by either testosterone or booze.

    Back then, we were just beginning our second decade. We had all known each other since kindergarten, and tonight was Halloween. We wanted the darkness to unleash the debauchery and depravity that we suspected was lurking inside each of us. (Hey, what can I say? Hope springs eternal.) But, back then, our 22-year-old bodies never needed any holiday to justify swilling down a few brewskis. Actually, to swill down a whole *lot* of brewskis!

    However, our holiday romp had turned into a bust. By the time we had crashed our way through three semi-boring parties by midnight, we were well along into powering through a case and a half of Bud Lite. Jimmy (who was by then on his umpteenth Pepsi), helped us chomp through three large Dominos pizzas with everything, including anchovies. Afterwards, the three boozers got back into the beer. No, the food didn't sober us up, of course, but at least we were now all well-fed drunks. It's truly amazing how much food you think you can eat when you're smashed. The good news was that nobody felt like they needed to hurl. Nothing can ruin your entire evening (to say nothing of a new car wash) than projectile vomiting at sixty miles an hour.

By that time, Jimmy had finally stopped sulking that, on All Hallows Eve, the Cosmos had randomly decided to grant him the unwelcomed gift of "temporary sobriety."

As the designated you-know-what, Jimmy's main function was to protect us from ourselves. This surprisingly mature idea for coverage had started a few months ago after another one of our marathon sessions with beer and Tequila. For some reason (actually, vomit was probably involved), we had pulled over on I-95 at 4:00 a.m., and one of us crazies had started kicking around a soccer ball in the fast lanes. Yikes! Funny as hell back then, but in the dawn's early light, we realized how lucky we were that we didn't get cited, much less killed.

After that, we decided that *someone* would have to be appointed the "Keeper-of-the-Keys" and to willingly witness the rest of us jerks voluntarily lowering our IQ's about ten points an hour. Since nobody ever volunteered to sit one out, we always let our fates be decided by the rock-paper-scissors gods, and, as I have noted, they had not smiled that holiday night on poor ole Jimbo.

Shortly after 1:00 a.m., Jimmy turned into the parking lot of Denny's to take a piss and pulled up next to a tricked-out pink Mercedes that we all instantly recognized. Yes. It was here, and, amazingly, *she* was sitting alone in it. Sharon LaRue herself. Our #1 high school hottie—all dressed up like she was auditioning for the next re-boot of *Girls Gone Wild*.

And she was smiling at us!

Blonde, bawdy, and totally blinged-out, that girl was *sparkling!* All the boys had wanted to jump her bones back in high school, and more than a few of them had given her a five-star rating in their little black books. To us guys, Sharon LaRue was an A-list kind of girl, but definitely one you never took home to mama.

As the only one of us who could walk, Jimmy went over to her car, leaving the rest of us babbling idiots trying to pull together what was left of our diminished faculties. Healthy guys our age are always out there trolling, and, even in an altered state, our hound-dog radars had quickly picked up the proximity of a willing female who was obviously available and on the prowl.

However, before they'd be willing to do the wild thing, we also knew that most girls first wanted the guys to be semi-coherent and to have their mojo up and running at full throttle. Sadly, none of us still fit that description. With all the beer and pizza, the boozer contingent in the back seat of the SUV that night was rapidly sliding downwards into sweet oblivion.

A few minutes later, Jimmy came back and told us that, yes, he had hooked up! He was going over to Sharon's house for a few hours of "R&R," but he'd return later to drive us all home after we'd slept it off.

"But, but..." I protested somewhat groggily, "you're supposed to stay here and protect us!"

"I *am* protecting you," he laughed. "See? I'm taking the keys."

"Wait, Jimbo! It's Sharon LaRue. And she's horny! Don't you want us to get laid, too?"

He smiled wickedly and said in a voice that was disgustingly sober, "Hey, buddy, that's not my job!"

Holidays, Again
Madalin Bickel

They are coming
not family and friends,
but the days that include
them at my table, in a house
that must be cleaned and
scrubbed so their allergies
won't kick in.

There will be food, lots of
food – turkey, cranberries, pies,
stuffing – it will cover the table
and everyone will dig in after the
proverbial prayer is said which
nobody will listen to no matter
how much we practice.

It should be about family and
thankfulness, and getting together
around a table rather than the
TV or some other electronic
gizmo.

In addition, they want to
hurry because Black Friday begins
on Brown Thursday. One thinks
the turkey was sacrificed for
nothing more than pre-Christmas
traditions that need to be
forgotten.

If the ground is shaking, it's the
Pilgrims quaking in their tombs
because a country, which days ago
swore their candidate would make
a difference, is once again more

concerned about spending money
than spending time with family
or thinking about our heritage. If
only we could turn back the clock
to when life was precious, simple,
and worth living.

A Thanksgiving Memory
Allita Irby

Waking to the aromas of
a roasting turkey with sage,
the house was filled with warmth,
my memory from an early age.

Spices filled the air like cinnamon
and nutmeg for pies,
visions of cakes and cookies for
wide little eyes.

'Twas a lasting memory
of Thanksgiving Day,
of family, of home, and hearth always.

WINTER

Potomac Winter Leaving
Elaine Lewis

Together we shuddered
At the furry wetness of
The river otter as it skittered
Through icy waters

The stone you threw after it
Clunked down the banks
To loosen long-frozen dark crystals
Into those strong currents

Silvered ice panes split the horizon
And glittered gulls and geese
As they dipped and dived
And yes - there were swans

Curling out their trumpet cries
Full feathered, white-winged
Earth angels sat, fanning
At sun-sheared winter skies

With mood-glazed eyes
I watched a low slow ship
Seeking skilled passage
Through rising river mists

Then I turned to find you - there
Snow-skipping through the trees
Your face shaped by sunlight
Dark hair lifting to the breeze

But then through carved marks
In tree trunks and table tops
You were seeing visions
Of another time

When, on these banks
Someone else stood
Here, near you

The History of a Fruitcake
C.A. Rowland

Flour flew as Marlene began whisking it with the macerated fruits and eggs. The pre-baking stage of soaking the fruit had been completed two days ago, but Marlene liked to think the first swipe of the whisk was the true beginning of her masterpiece.

Mixed together, the cake was just the right blend of fruit and rum, with Marlene's own special spices and secret ingredient. She knew a gift of fruitcake was likely to be ridiculed, at least at first, but her reputation for pies and more traditional cakes extended to the three surrounding counties. Why, she'd been the winner in the best homemade pie contest at the Sanderson County Fair three years running. Her baked goods were much sought after and she knew once word of her fruitcake got out, there'd be demand for it through the entire holiday season.

Craiseville was a small town of just under 10,000 people. It might seem big to some, but it was the kind of place where everyone knew everyone else's business. Marlene certainly made sure she knew what was going on due to how much she cared about Craiseville. After all, her ancestors had been one of the founding families.

As the fruitcake fermented, Marlene ruminated over who would properly appreciate the gift. She'd make others for her family as her annual contribution to each relative's family gathering. It was a tradition she loved even if it wasn't always valued as much as she thought it should be. For this first one, though, it would be given to someone in her own circle of friends. She only had to decide who would most enjoy it. She knew there was a special person who would love it.

Marlene wasn't sure when she first decided she wanted to make the concoction, but she'd dreamed about creating a setting of the graceful flamingos in the front yard as a December scene. A table in the middle would have food, but the star would be a fruitcake. Scarlett had insisted. Of course, she knew Scarlett, the matriarchal pink flamingo, couldn't really talk, but she'd learned to trust what she said in dreams. That must have been when she knew she was destined to make a perfect version. Thinking back, Marlene realized she hadn't given her friend Laura a homemade gift in years. While Laura hadn't said she wanted a sweet dessert, Marlene was sure she'd appreciate all the effort that went into making this particular loaf.

Marlene had changed the Thanksgiving costumes on the birds for more elf-like ones. They were complete with green clothing, bells and pointy hats, although Marlene hadn't had any red or gold fabric. She'd settled for a plaid left over from St. Patrick's Day but she didn't think anyone would really notice. Securing the hats was difficult so she simply added plaid ties that created a bow under the necks. With fabric to spare, she used the last of the plaid to secure the wrapping paper for the gift.

Presented with the package, Laura unwrapped the brightly colored paper and forced her mouth into a smile. She rolled the fabric ribbon into a ball, realizing the material was part of Marlene's flamingo family wardrobe. She'd dreaded this year, knowing Marlene always experimented with new recipes that she tried out on her friends. With twenty pounds to lose before the holidays, a fruitcake wasn't on her diet. Even if it had been, it was hardly a "treat" she would have asked for. She hated candied anything. Rum made her tongue break out in little blisters to the point she suspected she was allergic. Laura ran her hand through her blond curly hair—a nervous tick she hoped Marlene didn't notice.

"You'll love it," Marlene said. "It's my perfect recipe. Scarlett said so."

Laura stifled an urge to laugh. She wouldn't put fruitcake and perfect in the same sentence. And a flamingo who talked? It was all she could do not to roll her eyes as she said, "I'm sure we'll enjoy it. This was so thoughtful of you."

Laura knew it was the thought that counted, but she also knew her family wouldn't come within two feet of the cake. She resisted the urge to say so. She was loathe to throw it away. Marlene and she were friendly, but Marlene was also the town gossip. What if someone saw it in the trash? No, it would be better to pass it on. But what to do with it? Was this something that could be re-gifted? She realized if she didn't want it, no one else might either. Still, there must be someone she could give this to that was appropriate.

Prim and proper, with her straight auburn hair in a classic bun, Dorinda wasn't the obvious choice for the fruitcake. She straightened her shoulders and drew in a breath, exactly as she always did when facing a judge. The whole town knew she had her eye on the county commissioner position. She'd need all the votes she could get and couldn't afford to be offended, which Laura knew.

"I wanted to put any bad feelings behind us," Laura said as she delivered the re-wrapped gift with plaid bow.

Dorinda had represented the buyer of a piece of land Laura and her husband, Doug, were selling. The negotiations had been long and tedious. If it weren't for the fact her husband's brother was Dorinda's partner, Laura wouldn't have considered giving her anything. But family was family and it didn't hurt to know someone in power, if Dorinda was elected.

Dorinda hated to think about the meaning and motives behind the gift and certainly had no intention of eating the lump of doughy fruit in front of her. The real question was how many times this cake had been re-gifted. She knew Laura didn't bake. She also knew Laura was friends with Marlene. Marlene had cornered Dorinda at a local charity event and bent her ear about publishing a cookbook featuring her family history and her award-winning recipes.

"Picture this," Marlene had said. "We could include pictures of my flamingos for different holidays throughout."

Dorinda had conceded it was an interesting idea, but secretly doubted anyone would buy that type of book.

Dorinda decided her secretary, Debbie, was a safe bet for the gift. She'd add a gift certificate and a few other personal items so the fruitcake wasn't the main item. The last thing she wanted was for Debbie to feel slighted. A perfect solution.

Debbie looked at the fruitcake, crossed her arms and wondered if Dorinda had lost her mind. Who gave a fruitcake these days? Or any other time? Must have been a re-gifting. The fabric ribbon was a bit frayed –almost as if it had been tied before or used for something else. And plaid wasn't exactly a holiday fabric. She could have sworn she'd seen that fabric somewhere recently.

It wasn't as if Dorinda was a baker or cook. She was too busy in court and working long hours at the office. Eating it was out of the question. Debbie was a diabetic. That fact wasn't common knowledge and she'd never talked to Dorinda about it. Still, she hated to waste food with so many starving people in the world.

Debbie wondered who had made the cake. Had to be Marlene. She was the only one in town who would think that was a good idea. Normally

Debbie loved hearing what she had made and who had received it. She never dreamed she would be included. But no matter, she'd simply pass it on.

At the nursing home, the head nurse, Brenda, removed the fruitcake sitting on the table in front of Debbie's Aunt Judith. The nurse had promised to serve it to the residents, but most of their diets wouldn't allow for it. Since it was likely soaked in alcohol, she wasn't inclined to feed it to them anyway. Instead, she knew her son, Jake, liked sweets. She'd save it for him, just like she did with some of the "treats" Marlene brought the residents.

Brenda wasn't sure about some of the concoctions – strange cakes that included ingredients like sweet potatoes, lavender, Mountain Dew and green tea. All seemed to be inspired by someone named Scarlett that Marlene talked about. Brenda knew her heart was in the right place, but she just never seemed to consider the residents' restrictive diets. She wondered if the fruitcake was Marlene's. It didn't matter. The residents wouldn't ever know Brenda had not shared it with them. The ones who might, mostly likely wouldn't remember it had ever been there.

When Jake deposited the gift from his mom on the table, Hannah stared for a moment before asking, "What is that?"

"A fruitcake. Didn't you ever have one for the holidays?"

"I thought they were an urban legend. I've never actually seen one. What are we supposed to do with it?" Hannah asked.

Jake laughed. "Eat it, silly."

"Maybe you will, but I'll pass."

"I can't throw it out. One, it's from my mom and two, I'm a chef. We don't throw out perfectly good food."

Hannah's arched eyebrows gave voice to her question of whether the cake was really food, much less in the good category.

Jake and Hannah walked around the fruitcake for a few days. On Thursday evening, they watched an episode of Top Chef.

"That's it," he said jumping up.

Hannah stared at him. "What's it?"

"I know what to do with the fruitcake," Jake said as he paced the room.

The Jackson Inn had the only white tablecloth restaurant in Craiseville. Every year, the local book club reserved the private room for their holiday luncheon. In the past years, they had approved the menu in advance, but now they allowed the chef to choose for them. This year they were all reading several historical novels set in Rome and requested something suitable in the same theme.

Roast tuna was accompanied by Columella Salad, which their hostess assured them were each prepared in the culinary customs of ancient Rome. Jake brought the desserts in himself as he had the prior year.

Each creation rested along the center of an oblong white china plate.

"I know this is not something you expected, but I hope you enjoy it. I've created a deconstructed fruit cake with a vanilla rum crème. The nuts have been caramelized and the candied fruits serve as the garnish.

The ladies looked at each other and tentatively took their first bites. Shoulders relaxed. Conversation returned as the ladies lingered over the dessert. Even some of the foodies among them smiled as they waited for the president – the ultimate foodie in the group.

President Marlene took a bite. She had an excellent palate and she noted all the ingredients were the same as her recipe. Wondering where Jake's recipe came from, she took a second and third bite. This cake was yummy and certainly an inventive concoction. She knew her food and history. Fruitcake had begun in Rome.

"Very pleasing. And an appropriate dessert for the Roman inspired meal," she said to no one in particular.

Marlene would have to keep her eye on Jake. The fruitcake was quite good, and if his other baked goods were at the same level, she might have a real competitor for the Sanderson County fair events. The plating was excellent but the centerpiece on the main table caught her eye – a very nice fabric ribbon bow of green and red plaid. She wasn't sure that was strictly Roman, but thought she might take it home with her.

The bow could top the holiday tree for the flamingos.

She took another bite and savored the flavors melting in her mouth. The fruitcake was quite tasty, she thought, but the blend of spices was not quite right – it needed her secret ingredient. Otherwise it would have been perfect.

Previously published in A Readable Feast by Bethlehem Writers Group, LLC (November, 2015).

Always a Fresh Cut Tree at Christmas
Allita Irby

When we were at Grandmama's knee
She lived in a two room cabin, in the country.

One great room, with one door in
(the same door out).
A kitchen room to the left, with one door in
(the same door out).

The great room had a fireplace; the kitchen had
a wood stove.
The walls were wood and plaster and filled with
Love.

There was no running water, just a pump.
No refrigerator, just an ice box, you see.
At Christmas, always a fresh cut tree.

Many cows and chickens and hens from Guinea.
At Christmas, always a fresh cut tree.

For lights, oil lamps, no electricity
But at Christmas, always a fresh cut tree.

The Christmas Chronicles
jd young

During the holidays I always disliked getting yearly *summations* of people's lives. Not that I don't want to hear from them, but they generally finish their tomes in such a depressed state I'm forced to overdose on butter pecan ice cream.

The first sentence of their holiday note starts: "It has not been a good year. My wife had three surgeries, my son was in a skiing accident, I lost my job..." and ends with a jolly, "ya'll have a wonderful holiday season."

The sender will only commit to one sheet of paper and therefore prints the tome in 8pt type which looks like ground pepper on a green and red poinsettia-laden background. You end up reading the first sentence, skim down the page and finish with a long sigh.

I decided to follow suit by sending holiday letters. My therapist felt it would be more relaxing than basket weaving and a lot healthier than Level 2 narcotics. I felt my sending these tomes was payback for the years of death and destruction visited upon me by my friends.

* * *

HAPPY MERRY HOLIDAY CHRISTMAS

For those of you that know me – okay, everyone on this list – I've decided a *Welcome January/Let's Celebrate 1st Quarter/New Year Note* is what I can handle at the moment. At least I'm not writing from St. Elizabeth's Hospital for the Neglected Menopausal Boomer – on the other hand – can you be sure? Really, they promised my November release was permanent this time.

Yup, yup, yup we ended the year and started this one with Christmas, Hanukah, Kwanzaa, New Year's, Ramadan, Winter Solstice, Boxing Day, Epiphany, St. Lucia Day (watch "The Ref" for info on this little recognized holiday - it is priceless) and my particular favorite, Penguin Awareness Day, celebrated on January 20th. Whichever you celebrate(d) hope it was good, you received lots of presents, food out the yang and a major gain in your 401(k).

Thankfully we have a few years till the Mayan calendar warns we will be hit by an asteroid of such monumental proportions that our tiny earth bottoms will explode into dust particles. Just my destiny – I'll be Bronx dandruff on the rings of Saturn. Earth will be obliterated and life will end, all because the Mayans got writer's cramp and didn't finish the calendar. How can we be sure it wasn't a big joke by some medicine man with a warped sense of humor and one too many puffs on magic leaves? Maybe Mayan specters are loitering around the clouds laughing their interim wings off because we give this any sort of credence.

You were thinking what – this year your kids would be out of college and out of your house, you might be retired, the cars and home paid for, no worries – right? In the immortal words of Tony Soprano ... ahhhh, you know what those words are!

Christmas was quiet. Jerry and I were alone. Okay, maybe it could have been better. However, company did come. Peggy and Jimmy arrived two days prior to New Years; Rosie and Casey followed. I love company because I like to feed them. I love to cook. I yearn for visitors' hips to rival my Rubenesque form. I was thinking lasagna, stuffed manicotti, turkey and dressing, cheesecake. Then I found out: Peggy was on Weight Watchers, Jimmy didn't like onions, Rosie was diagnosed with Celiac disease (severe allergy to wheat, rye and barley) and Casey was a Vegan.

My menu choices spiraled downward. I stocked up on: skim milk, soy milk, 2% milk, yogurt butter, spray butter (it is approved by FDA), cucumbers, spinach, yogurt with live cultures, yogurt with semi-something cultures, spelt bread and anything raw in the veggie case. On the plus side of the universe, I only required a case of wine and my faithful butter pecan.

I queried the Food Network on a variety of creative, tasteful and appropriate menus – broiled placemats, filet of substance found on road, crème de la (oh, I can't share that one!) My heart pounded for three days trying to determine menus. I did an Excel spreadsheet. I purchased every bit of fresh fruit in my zip code, hoarded seltzer, bottled water and real juice. I made fresh vinaigrettes, salads, and salsa. I made two kinds of stew – one veggie – one with beef, but no gravy thickener or onions.

I had rolls at one end of the table and spelt bread at the other, real butter, yogurt butter, spray butter, juice, milk, water, seltzer, beer, wine, soda, coffee, tea (hot and cold.) I did dishes non-stop and ran out of pans to cook with (and you know how many I own!)

All went off without a major hitch, and by New Year's Eve all had gone and Jerry and I were left with a major decision – watch the ball drop or go to bed. Bed won out. I guess I am getting older.

Our best to each of you for a peaceful, quiet and blessed New Year.

Love ya, Scarlett

* * *

HAPPY MERRY HOLIDAY CHRISTMAS

Hope all is well with you, the kids, the businesses, the retirements. I can't believe the year has passed so quickly – yada, yada, yada – boring. I just figured it was a fitting way to start the next chapter of this narrative. This year has been quiet and uneventful; I also have some pristine waterfront property in Jersey that may interest you. Badda Bing (too much?)

Anyway, the year arrived quietly, a thoroughly refreshing occurrence for me. Work was slow, no immediate emergency room visits, all the cars were functioning and the IRS hadn't gotten around to dunning me for yet another year of back taxes. What with the Beamers, diamond bracelets and health insurance premiums, who has change left for the government?

Jerry started the year by having a small procedure. Health insurance identified it as surgery, but he dislikes the word so I humor him. He had a small 'thing' removed from the side of his nose. Twelve stitches and a 1½ inch half scar, but he still rocks my world and is now in great health. He so looked like Dennis Farina in *Get Shorty*. His knees are doing beautifully – not a candidate for Cirque de Soleil, but maybe a short stint at Ice Capades. He has forgone Spanish at work and has adopted Russian as his second language. Nothing quite as sexy as a West Virginia farm boy blurting: Вы потеряли Холодную войну - возвращаются, чтобы работать - Ya'll! You lost the Cold War – go back to work – Ya'll.

Rosie was promoted to Catering Chef and transferred from the The Inn to The Summers Restaurant – am told it is a fabulous eatery. When I have the triple platinum credit card required to have dinner there, I will let you know. She is going to Marseilles for her Christmas vacation and will be spending the summer in the South of France. Am sure Kings Island was her second choice. If I were taller, blonder, flat-chested and had a space between my front teeth, I'd be living there too. Rosie opted for an exciting Thanksgiving by inviting the family to spend nine hours in the GW emergency room. Thankfully not an accident with her chef's knife. Her choice this year was pneumonia, but she has recovered nicely. I don't believe the ER doctor that tended her will send me a holiday card. I have no idea why he bristled at my suggestions for breaking her 104° temperature. After all, she lived in my house for eighteen years – where was he?

Wynonna had her car bruised only once this year – the air bags exploded without warning in a parking garage. After they exploded she couldn't see and thankfully missed the Corvette, but bumped the retaining wall. That was way exciting. A quick trip to the ER and a $4k claim for new airbags started her and the insurance carrier's year off spectacularly. Only one hospital visit for her this year for an ulcer that perforated. You would think that after spending the major portion of her life in our household, stress would manifest as mere annoyance! She is gainfully employed as a tech analyst and does something with a computer and its language. I guess they talk now. It's a blessing to be oblivious to the technology around me. I'm happy with a Kitchenaid and unbleached flour.

Scarlett – well, my hips have continued to expand, my chin has gracefully repositioned on my collarbone and my arms have wholly filled my new "mature woman" sized blouse. Color me full-filled and working on contentment. No hospital visits for me, but am stocking up on

Sports Cream and something called Blue Emu Oil for my newly visiting arthritis and, no, I don't care how they get the oil from the emu.

I no longer chase the FedEx man to Dulles airport worrying about some CEO getting his golden parachute, golden handcuffs or outrageous compensation package. I no longer fret about incomplete PowerPoint presentations, Fed Ex packages or consultants proffering writing advice when they cannot string together two sentences without the editorial aid of their assistants.

We are happy and healthy – or at least making a valiant effort. May God Bless us all and continue covering us with His Grace.

Love ya, Scarlett

Home for the Holidays
Julie Phend

Oh, there's no place like home for the holidays.

The song ran through my head like a mantra. Home for the holidays. That's what I wanted for Christmas.

"That's *really* what you want?" my husband asked, shaking his head.

I nodded. "That's *all* I want."

"That's really all you want?" my mom asked when I told her over the phone. And then my mother-in-law.

Yes. That's what I wanted. A trip home for the three of us: myself, my husband, Jack, and our baby girl, Jenny, who would turn one on December 20th.

We had been living in southwest Virginia since before the baby was born, but all our relatives, including both sets of grandparents, lived in the upper Midwest. Driving there with a one-year-old was impossible in the winter, and flying would break our meager budget. My proposal was that our parents could pitch in and give us the trip as our only Christmas gift.

Of course they agreed, thrilled at the idea of introducing Jenny to her first old-fashioned family Christmas.

I couldn't wait to take my baby home for the holidays. She'd have a Christmas like those of my childhood. With a fresh-cut tree tall enough to touch the living room ceiling decorated with glass balls, colored lights, and a rainfall of tinsel. Mountains of presents and loads of relatives. Platters piled high with Christmas delicacies and homemade cookies. With the whisper of secrets and the joy of surprises. The beauty of snow at midnight on Christmas Eve. Yes, I wanted my daughter to experience it all.

We planned everything perfectly. We would leave on Jenny's first birthday, fly to Chicago and then to the small regional airport near Wausau, Wisconsin, where my parents lived. We'd spend Christmas with them and all my siblings, who were traveling shorter distances to be with us. After Christmas, we'd fly to Indiana and spend a week with Jack's family, celebrating a second Christmas and New Year's Eve with them.

I got busy making lists, packing everything we could possibly need: bottles and blankets, diapers and Desitin, toys and toiletries, warm sweaters, boots, hats, scarves, and mittens, festive outfits and gifts galore. I planned for every eventuality.

Or so I thought.

On the morning of our flight, a neighbor drove us to the airport. Juggling baby and bags, we headed to check-in. The airport was packed; the lines were long. Jenny started to cry. I jiggled her up and down, trying to calm her.

She cried louder. She screamed. She wailed.

"Sorry," I whispered to the others in line. "Sorry. Sorry."

And then she threw up.

Not spit up. She *threw* up. Great gooey chunks of milky mess. All over me. All over her.

I panicked. This had never happened before. What was wrong? What should we do? Could we fly?

Jack said yes, she was probably just over-excited.

Jenny kept screaming.

I was attacked by the *what-ifs*. "I have to call the pediatrician," I announced.

Wiping at the front of my stinky coat with a soggy tissue, I went in search of a pay phone (ah, the days before cell phones) leaving Jack to juggle baby, bags, and annoyed passengers.

Have I mentioned that the airport was crowded?

It took forever to find a phone and then to stand in line. But I finally reached the pediatrician. He agreed with Jack. Jenny was probably over-stimulated. Plus, her stomach might be upset by the birthday cake she'd eaten the day before.

"Try to keep her calm," he suggested, "and don't feed her. She'll do better on an empty stomach."

Relieved, I found my way back to my haggard husband. We handed over our luggage, grabbed our boarding passes, and rushed to the gate. We barely made it, but at last we were on board—headed home for the holidays.

Or so we thought.

We hadn't bought a seat for the baby, planning to hold her during the flight. Of course, that meant there was a stranger occupying the third seat of our row. A very upright, prim and proper man. When I sat down, he took one whiff, pulled out a handkerchief and covered his nose, looking at me with an expression of distaste.

I glanced down at the chunks congealing on my coat and cringed. "Sorry," I said. "She got sick."

He turned his head away, staring glumly out the window.

The plane took off. Jenny screamed.

And then she threw up again.

That was when I understood what it means to be a mother. Off the ground without a manual and in it for the long haul.

The flight was awful. Jenny cried and cried. I pulled out her favorite book, the one that never failed to bring a smile, but she pushed it away. Jack dangled toys, and I whispered rhymes. We rocked her, hugged her, sang to her. But Jenny would not be comforted. I couldn't even offer the solace of nursing or a cracker—doctor's orders. Jack and I endured her tears, the tiny seats and dirty looks, counting the minutes until we would land in Chicago.

Not long now. At least we could get out of this confined space and walk around. Maybe that would comfort our baby.

The seatbelt sign came on, and the pilot informed us that there was a snowstorm in

Chicago. Flights were backed up. We would be circling until he got clearance to land.

The plane circled.

Jenny cried. The plane circled.

I prayed. The plane circled.

Would we never land?

The loudspeaker crackled and we heard the pilot's voice. Finally.

But, no. "We still are not cleared for landing," he said. "And we are low on fuel. We are going to Cincinnati to refuel."

Jack put his face in his hands. So did the man on the other side of me.

But at least we were landing *somewhere*.

At the airport in Cincinnati, we paced the halls. We bought something to eat and, God help me, I fed my baby. Forget doctor's orders—she must be starving, I reasoned.

For a few blessed minutes, Jenny stopped crying. Her eyelids fluttered shut, and her little body relaxed. I breathed a bit easier.

The loudspeaker crackled to life. It was time to re-board.

On cue, Jenny woke up.

And threw up. And started crying again.

I was beside myself with guilt and fear. I shouldn't have fed her. But what was wrong? Her face was flushed. Was it from crying, or did she have a fever? I had no thermometer, no way to know. Maybe it was stomach flu? Or something even more serious?

Tired, stinky, crabby, and worried, we got back on the plane and circled some more.

Eventually, we did land in Chicago. But it was still snowing, and by then, we had missed our connecting flight. So had everybody else. Lines were long, people were cranky, and Jenny was still crying.

By some miracle, we were able to fly out late that night. It was almost midnight when my dad picked us up at the airport, bundled to the teeth against the frigid weather. We drove over icy roads through a blinding blizzard on the final leg of that awful journey.

And then at last, we were on my parents' street. I could see the twinkling lights of the tree through the living room window. We were home for the holidays!

But the next day, Jenny was still sick. And so were we. Really sick. (Turns out she wasn't just overexcited after all.)

My poor mom had to take care of all three of us. For days. In the midst of her Christmas preparations. (That's what it is to be a mom—in it for the long haul.)

Christmas was a blur. I barely remember it—too sick to see my siblings or enjoy the holiday I'd so looked forward to. But Jenny had recovered, and was crawling around enjoying the fuss. (Presumably, she enjoyed more of the holiday than I did.)

By the end of the week, we were well enough to travel again. And this time it wasn't snowing. Things were looking up.

We were going to Jack's home for the rest of the holidays. We'd have a real Christmas there.

Or so I thought.

We said our good-byes and climbed aboard the tiniest plane I'd ever seen—just eight passenger seats, four on each side of the plane. My heart was in my mouth as we took off, but Jenny just giggled and begged for a story. (Who can figure out a kid?) The flight was actually fine—except for the part where we had to duck all the huge planes at O'Hare.

Jack's dad picked us up at the airport. "Betty is really looking forward to seeing you," he declared. "Been preparing all week!"

But when we opened the back door, Betty was nowhere in sight. We called out a greeting, expecting her to come flying in to fuss over the baby.

There was only silence.

And then we found the note on the bedroom door.

She was sick.

Really sick!

Betty did not emerge from the bedroom the whole week we were there—too afraid of infecting us or the baby. (That's what it is to be a mom—willing to give up your Christmas to protect others.)

Needless to say, our celebrations were subdued. No guests. No parties. No elaborate dinners. Just the three of us, Jack, and Elmer and me, ordering pizza and watching the ball drop on New Year's Eve.

Still, watching our *healthy* baby crawl around the Christmas tree, I knew I was blessed.

No, there's no place like home for the holidays.

But ever since that fateful trip, I *stay* home.

Third Grade Christmas, 1953
W. Rosser Wilson

I'm counting the minutes, 29 to go 'til the bell rings and we're out on Christmas break. Miss Ballard, she keeps reading aloud "The Dancing Snowmen," not wanting to waste a minute of quality time with the class. It's a story for babies. We're third graders!

Next thing I know, Frank Orndorf, the kid behind me, taps me on the shoulder.

I jump out of my chair. Last week he tapped my shoulder just before he splashed puke all over the floor next to my desk.

Miss Ballard, she stops reading and gives me "the stare." It could stop a train.

No puke, so I sit back down. Two seconds later, Orndorf kicks my chair. I turn around and he's got a big gotcha grin.

"Hey Billy, did you know there's no Santa Claus? Your parents put the stuff in your stocking. He's a fake."

Orndorf lives on a farm and milks cows and stuff. That makes him an expert? And besides, he decides to tell me this two days before Christmas?

"You're wrong, Orndorf. My Dad and I found out last year he's real. We made an experiment and caught him, but he got away." I give him a Miss Ballard stare and pack up my stuff to go.

It's snowing by the time we are let out and I walk home. I push open the door and smell gingerbread. My smart-aleck eighth-grade sister, big deal, is baking cookies.

Mom calls, "Wipe your feet." And then she asks, "How was school?"

"Good." What else do you say to something stupid like that? I tell her Frank Orndorf told me there's no Santa Claus.

She wipes her hands on her apron, makes a sigh, and nods toward the living room. "Your father's home. They're putting snowplows on the front of the garbage trucks. Be quiet, he's resting. They'll be calling him back to plow as soon as there's two inches."

"Billy, come in here," Dad shouts. As I walk in the room, he puts down his beer and mutes the TV. "Did I hear you tell your mother Frank Orndorf said there's no Santa? Did you tell him how we proved he was real? How we pulled the washing machine off the porch into the living room, put it in front of the fireplace, and turned on the wringer—and in the morning you had a bunch of toys in the tub and half his beard in the wringer?"

I couldn't tell my Dad I'm sorry we did that, because I'm scared Santa will remember the house and skip us this year.

"Dad, tell him the truth!" My sister screams from the kitchen. "Billy, that was an old mop in the wringer! There's no Santa Claus."

She's real smart, got a scholarship to a Catholic school and for them lying is a big sin. She's got to be telling the truth or she'll go to you-know-where. I don't actually mind believing

110

there's no Santa as long as the presents keep coming. But I mind that a jerk like Orndorf was right.

Then she says, "The nuns believe Saint Nicholas is the spirit of giving to others, especially kindness and peace."

I guess the nuns are right too. So, Merry Christmas anyway. Billy

A Christmas Story: Benson's Letter to Grandma and Granddad
Major General Mari K. Eder, U.S. Army (Retired)

Dear Grandma and Granddad,

I hope you both had a very happy Christmas. Mama said I should say thank you for the new coat. I didn't need a new coat. I can grow my own. But she said I have enough toys and I don't need any new ones. I am glad you sent me some toys anyway. And the bacon-flavored treats are yummy. I did share too. Maggie got one and I got three. That is pretty even I think because she is smaller than me.

Besides, she is still in trouble with Mama. I promised not to tell but I can tell you. You know that sometimes Maggie will stick her long snout in the back door and open it. Then she hops out and away she goes. She doesn't really run away. Maggie told me once that when she was a puppy she lived in a house with mean people. But they did have a fenced yard and she could roam around it all she wanted. So that was okay with her. But we don't have a fenced yard so she trots along until she sees a fence and then she turns back for home.

But this time it didn't happen. It was Christmas Eve and it had been raining all day. Maggie didn't want to go out for a walk even though she had been chewing on her bacon treat and drinking a lot of water. I knew she had to go. Her little cheeks even looked full and her eyes bugged out. But she didn't want to get her toes wet. So she crossed her little doggie legs and waited. It was about four o'clock when Mama came in with the mail. I ran to look in case there were any more gift boxes for me. That is when Maggie snuck out the door.

Now you know why I call her the evil Moo! She is sneaky and as fast as a fox. It wasn't really raining much by then, but it was very misty and foggy. By the time Mama had put the mail down on the table she had hopped away into the neighbor's yard to do her business. So Mama pulled on her good raincoat with the hood and ran out the door calling Maggie's name.

I stayed inside like the good boy that I am and ate the rest of her bacon cookie. I didn't think she would miss it. And Mama was outside so I didn't get caught.

About twenty minutes later, Mama came back but without the Moo! Then she asked Auntie Debra to go drive around the neighborhood while she walked along the lake behind all the neighbor's houses. You remember we live on the lake now, right? It was getting dark and I know Maggie wouldn't go near the water. Plus, she was looking for the fence. But what if in the fog, she missed it? She would probably keep going until the end of the world and then make a U-turn. I bet Mama was worried about that too.

Anyway, Auntie Debra took me along with her in the truck and told me to keep a sharp lookout. I am a very good guard dog and a secret spy too. But it was sure getting dark and, when the wind blew, all of that wet, lumpy fog just looked like thick smoke. It worked just like an invisibility cloak. After all, a silver Schnauzer can go invisible much easier than a salt and pepper beast, like that Moo. Even so, she would have been nearly invisible in all that fog and drizzle.

I still kept looking. And so we drove very slowly around and around all of the side streets. Sometimes I could see a soft glow swinging back and forth in the distance and I knew that was Mama, shining her flashlight in the bushes and calling Maggie's name. Then Auntie Debra went around a corner and we had to back up so we could come around the circle one more time.

My window was down so I could sniff for clues and listen for Mama if she called me for help. But all I could smell was wet dog – and that was me. Suddenly I heard Mama yell, "I'm coming, Maggie! Mama's coming!" I barked out an alert to Auntie Debra and she hit the gas. We swung around the corner, just in time to catch a glimpse of Mama's raincoat as she flew down one of the neighbors' driveways. Auntie Debra turned into the driveway and put on the bright headlights.

Just then I saw Mama jump over the neighbor's dock and into the water. There was a big splash, then Mama disappeared! Auntie Debra shrieked and stopped the car. She opened the door and we both jumped out, racing ahead to the dock. Good thing nobody was home in that house. I think they went to Florida for the holidays and their boat was in storage. But their yard was all downhill and muddy and I slipped and slid all the way to the edge of the dark dock. The water looked black. By now it was dusk and you couldn't see much but moving shadows. But Auntie Debra peered over the end of the dock and there was Mama.

Mama was standing in waist-deep water, holding a soaked and bedraggled Maggie Moo in her arms. Maggie was making little squeaky, shivering noises and crying. That water must have been really cold. She was shaking and sounded very pitiful. I almost felt guilty for eating her treat. Almost.

Auntie Debra drove us straight home. Mama pulled on a dry pair of sweat pants and shoes, then we all hopped back in the car and drove straight to the vet's office. Yes, they were still open, just finishing up their last minute office chores and getting ready to head home for the holidays. Mrs. Vet was there too; it was her day to stay late. When Mama called and told her that Maggie had nearly drowned, she put down her coat and kept the door open for us.

So in we went. Mrs. Vet checked Maggie out and made sure she didn't have any broken bones. She was still whimpering and crying so they covered her with warm towels in the back room to get her to stop shaking. I stayed with the nice office girls in the front, munching on their Christmas cookies. Not bad, but the sprinkles get stuck in my teeth sometimes.

While we were waiting, Mr. Vet called in to see how Maggie was doing. Then he asked Mrs. Vet if Mama was all right. Tee Hee. I guess Mama doesn't have to do the Polar Bear challenge this year. Don't ask me why they do it, but that's when people jump into the cold water on New Year's Day. Sometimes humans do the silliest things.

Anyway, Auntie Debra was wringing her hands and Mama was pacing back and forth. Her hair was still wet and she smelled a lot like mud and a little like dead fish. Even Mrs. Vet wrinkled her nose at Mama. But while everyone was very worried, that Moo was just fine. That little dog has more lives than a cat, I swear. Since I didn't want to smell Mama any more, I put my paw on the receptionist's lap and gave her the big brown eyed stare. She handed over another cookie. It works every time.

About twenty minutes later, Maggie came prancing out like she had been having her nails done at the spa and everyone was happy to see her wag her little nub tail. I have to admit, Grandma, that I was worried a little bit too. And I was even glad to see that she was just fine.

Maggie told me later what happened. She did hop over into the neighbor's yard to do her business. She has a favorite bush there by the corner of their house. Then the fog got very low and the wind started blowing. Maggie got lost. It was quiet and all the neighbor people and dogs were inside. She kept looking for that fence and trotting along. She must have missed it somehow. Then she ended up at the far end of the street. She had never been that far alone, and certainly not in the dark. Then she fell in the water.

Schnauzers don't swim. You know we don't have the right padded paws. Not like I would ever go into water voluntarily anyway. That is too much like a bath. So Maggie just clung to the bulkhead and barked for Mama to come save her. She said she never had any doubt Mama would come. Mama would never leave her alone, out in the cold.

So, I am actually proud of my little sister, the Moo. She did get in trouble, but she sure didn't mean to. She fell in the lake but she hung on for dear life. And she never stopped believing. For once she taught me something too, never give up. I know I can always count on Mama. And Auntie Debra. And Maggie Moo. Maybe I will even give her my last bacon treat tomorrow. I think she earned it.

Love,
Benson

Author's note: Benson is a Miniature Schnauzer with a talent for trouble and telling tall tales about his adventures. He has published two books of his stories, 1001 Places to Pee Before You Die and Party Pooper. Both are available on Amazon.

A Colonial Farm Christmas
J. Allen Hill
Excerpted from *The Cause, the Odyssey of Daniel Grant*, a novel by J. Allen Hill

Deer Valley, Virginia. December 25, 1774... Daniel Grant woke early, his breath suspended in the cold dark air of the sleeping loft. He loved this time of this day because all was before him and he did not want to rush it along. He knew a blanket of stars still crowned the valley from horizon to horizon, and that overnight new snow had buried the valley in white. Birds slept in their nests, heads tucked beneath their wings. The cows stood patiently in the barn waiting to be milked but had not yet begun to low. On this day the air was charged with the promise of exciting things to happen. He believed it must borrow that feeling from the first day, the Child's birthday. The valley knew. He thought the whole world must know. This day was Christmas.

"Daniel," his father bellowed from below. "Get to the milking."

Then again, some things never change, even on Christmas.

* * *

As Daniel waded in deep snow to the barn, he waved to guests arriving from across the valley, their sleighs decked with bells for the day. Neighbor Hugh Anderson drove from the high bench seat, his wife Martha by his side. Their three boys and two visitors sat bundled beneath quilts in the wagon box. Silas Cartwright, the local traveling peddler followed after, his wagon full of the promise of extra treats, puzzles, and games.

"Come on, Red One, you lazy lump," Daniel scolded the large red cow. "Hurry up and give! I am missing all the fun." Her sister, Red Two spent the time slapping Daniel with her tail, but to her credit, filled her bucket of milk in minutes. When both had given their all, Daniel ran toward the spring house buckets in hand, milk sloshing and spilling into the snow.

Suddenly, a shout of, "Fight! Fight!" rang out and snowballs pelted Daniel from all sides. Setting the milk pails into a drift he tried to return fire. It was the three Anderson boys and his brother William against Daniel, and Daniel was losing. Covered in snow, eating it, blind with it, he collapsed laughing into the deeps of it.

"Boys," called Daniel's mother, Elsa. "Stop the rough housin'. Time tae come in."

"Coming Ma, soon's we take the milk to the spring house."

Everyone helped, but search as they might, the boys could not find the milk buckets until William fell over one and hit his head on the other. Both buckets were entirely filled with snow.

"Gor! What we gonna do now?" worried Daniel and the Anderson boys.

But little William was already up and running toward the house shouting, "Ma, guess what Dan'l did. He done ruin't the milk."

Daniel's father roared from the house, switch in hand, Christmas smile wiped from his face.

"Findley Grant!" Elsa's sharp command stopped the man before he could reach the silent boys.

"Dinnae touch the boy! Bring the buckets tae me, snow an' aw. And dinnae spill a drop."

Daniel and Carter Anderson, heads hung low, carried the milk-and-snow-filled buckets to the house where Elsa was handing out spoons all around.

"Set the pails on the table," she said, as she poured ladles of dark rich honey and walnuts into each one. "Gaither roon, everyone. 'Tis snow ice cream. We shall have dessert first this Christmas."

So went the rest of the day. Backwards. After filling up on the sweet treat, no one was hungry for Christmas dinner.

Turkey pies went into a warming oven, roast venison was moved from the fire. The kettle of vegetables in butter and broth went uncooked. Out came the cider and brew, the toys and games, men's pipes, women's knitting. The talk was of crops and cows, memories of the homeland, rude mockery of the Crown. Laughter and tumult filled the room until glasses were emptied, the fire was banked and peace descended.

Though coming days might hold hunger and pain, terror and death, that day was a memory Daniel would hold for the rest of his life.

Our Three Hour Tour, Christmas Surprise
Carol Zacheis

Did you ever wonder how you would get all your Christmas shopping done in time? How about those decisions regarding what to get each person on your list? Do you ever question if the person you were trying so hard to please would even remember what you finally gave them?

Let's move on to something we do know.

I'll take a wild guess that you can already imagine what the repercussions would be if your family had to give up their electronic gadgets for just three hours. That bad, huh? Well, let me help you out with a couple of Christmas related surprises that I never saw coming.

It all started a few years ago, when someone had the bright idea of giving us the 'gift' of a three-hour boat rental. The fine print on the gift certificate explained, in microscopic letters, that it must be used on the 23 of December, or as we like to call it, Christmas Eve Eve. I'm quite sure the benefactor in question had only our best interests at heart. I mean, nobody 're-gifts' a 3-hour boat rental — do they?

Well, let me tell you, there was no way that I had any time to spare leading up to Christmas. I still had baking, shopping, wrapping, and decorating to do. The preparation for my annual Christmas Eve gathering before the candlelight service at church was daunting, to say the least. I always liked to have things just right, even if it nearly killed me, so naturally, I never intended to go on this boat thing.

However, my family, who didn't have anything better to do, insisted that it would 'be fun'. They pulled that 'let's take a vote' stunt on me. Of course in the end, I relented and soon found myself packed in the SUV on our way to embark on a three hour boat ride two days before Christmas.

I glanced over at my husband, Joe, and started to relax, looking forward to this special time with my family. I peeked back at my marvelous children, with the expectation of seeing them happily excited about this fun escapade they had campaigned so extensively for. Instead, I saw Alex, our twelve-year-old, with his head down, his eyes glued to the screen of the game he was playing, and his thumbs working a mile a minute.

Sophia, who had recently turned eleven, was equally engrossed, with her head phones over her ears, watching a movie. Her attention didn't deviate one iota from her engrossing monitor. She had checked out from all human interaction by activating her cone of silence and engaging her 'do not disturb shield.' She was now in a fully inaccessible mode.

Neither of my kids seemed aware of anything except their gadgets. I can't explain how sad and melancholy this made me feel. I missed them, even though they were right in front of me.

When we arrived at the rental pier, the only boat that was not already in dry dock was timeworn. It had a wheelhouse on a platform and the equipment looked dilapidated. Truth be told, the boat appeared just plain worn out. The only worthwhile thing about it was the giant brass and wood steering wheel with spokes. Rick, the rental agent, informed us it was positively seaworthy; however, no one could take any electronic devises onboard because it might cause the equipment to malfunction. That's right. I'm talking about those very things that seemed to be as necessary to my children as air to breathe.

Now it was their turn to feel shook up as they sadly walked back to the vehicle to deposit their paraphernalia. The separation process from all those offending devices was definitely painful. The kids actually looked traumatized as we gathered back by the boat.

While this was going on, Joe had been working with Rick to get the boat started. When nothing seemed successful, Rick went to get some additional gas, to see if it might be low on fuel.

Joe asked the kids to make sure the life jackets were in good condition. They looked down below and found them.

"Hey Dad, these seem to be in better shape than this boat," exclaimed Alex as he carried them up.

Soon Rick returned with some gas. He and Joe continued to try to start the old vessel, until, at last, the sputtering motor took hold. However, now Joe and I hesitated as we exchanged looks that indicated this might not be a good idea after all.

Rick realized he might need to sweeten the deal, so he said, "Look, we close in about half an hour. I'm going to lock up and we won't reopen until the week after New Year's." With the kids looking hopeful, he added, "You're welcome to use the boat for as long as you like. Only tie and lock it up here at the dock when you're done."

"Great! We'll take it," said Joe with a smile.

"Okay, everyone, cheer up. Let's have some fun," I called as we climbed aboard the forlorn boat.

With no time limits, we decided to go all the way out to a couple of the barrier islands along the coast. It took us a while to get there, but the trip was worth it.

We were amazed by the beautiful scenery, and as we approached one of the islands, a lighthouse came into view. We drew closer to get a better look, and waved back and forth with two kids on the shore. They were busy working with a shovel and appeared to be digging up clams.

This was about the same time we discovered that our 'seaworthy boat,' had officially given up the ghost and abruptly stopped running.

The lighthouse keeper, who had seen our trouble, came to our aid immediately. He threw us a rope and proceeded to pull us safely to shore. I'll never forget his welcoming smile as he said, "Hi, I'm Ben."

"Wow, I appreciate what you did for us," said Joe with relief. The men shook hands as my husband continued, "Thanks, I'm not sure what we would have done without you! This is my wife, and my kids, Alex and Sophia."

"Glad I could be of help. That's what I'm trained for. These two ragamuffins are my children, Kevin and Mia," Ben laughed.

Mia smiled and shyly hung onto her dad's arm as she objected, "We're not ragamuffins."

Kevin had been chewing on a piece of straw and assessing the situation, as only a young teenager can do. "What happened to your boat? Did you run out of gas?"

"I'm not sure, but we had quite a bit of trouble starting it today," explained Joe. "It did look questionable, but the rental man assured us it was definitely seaworthy. I guess he was wrong."

Ben frowned at the boat. "There is no way to get you back to the mainland until after Christmas. In the meantime, we have ample room and food to put you up." He sounded as if we'd just dropped in for a cup of tea.

He invited us to the keeper's cottage to meet his wife, Sara. She was very attractive and as good-natured as her husband. She asked if anyone had been hurt, then happily showed us the cottage, and the extra sleeping areas for us. Her calm sincere attitude led me to believe this was somehow normal for them.

To my utter amazement, she said, "I hope you folks are hungry because we are having a clam bake down on the beach. By the way, kids, how is the clam digging project coming?"

"Well, I'm starving," laughed Kevin. "So I guess we need a few more!" He turned to Alex. "You want to help?"

Alex smiled. "Sure."

"Hey, wait for me," cried Mia, as she signaled to Sophia to join her and started running after the boys.

Later, I was astonished to watch our children pitch in and help dig out the fire pit. They actually seemed to be having fun as they gathered seaweed, driftwood and smooth rocks for the fire.

The lighthouse family had designed some permanent seating surrounding the pit area by using logs and a couple of huge boulders. These delightful people seemed authentically suited for their life. But what truly surprised me most was the fact that, in this strange setting, my family did too.

The clam bake tasted like the best seafood I had ever eaten. As we relaxed around the campfire, we saw a spectacular orange and pink sunset over the ocean. It felt like we had somehow formed a bond, or an unexpected connection, with this family. Our kids were about the same ages and they quickly became fast friends.

The stars appeared in the night sky while we sat around a fire and made smores. I could hardly believe it as I sat there trying to remember when I had even ten minutes to sit down, to say nothing of hanging-out, on Christmas Eve Eve. It occurred to me the better question was when had I ever made time to relax and enjoy happy moments with my family this close to Christmas?

As the stars grew brighter, we heard Kevin pointing out the North Star and the Big Dipper. He also wondered aloud if that was the star the shepherds saw in the sky on Christmas. Ben shared the fact that the sea captains of old used the stars to guide their ships. The lighthouse family had a vast amount of knowledge about the stars.

Meanwhile, I was starting to feel some remorse about my lack of spending quality time with my family at Christmas, despite the fact that I wore myself out striving to be the best Christmas Hostess in the area. I had always insisted that we be part of the Christmas Home Tour each year, and this was a huge inconvenience for the whole family.

I suddenly remembered about tomorrow's Christmas Eve gathering, scheduled to take place at my house. Now my conscience was starting to bother me big time, as I admitted that this event took priority over my family. This extravaganza was the highlight of Christmas Eve.

The long buffet table was strategically arranged to show off its stunning ice sculpture centerpiece with flowing ribbons, soft candles, and beautiful flowers. This was, of course, surrounded by an extensive spread of delicious food. The dessert table alone was staged to display an array of crowd-pleasing treats which included all the classic favorites, as well as an ice cream bar.

The house decorations for this event, both inside and out, were warm and inviting. Literally everything, right down to the beautiful ribbons and bows on the presents under the tree resembled an elegant work of art.

But what did all my efforts have to do with the real meaning of Christmas? Whoa, I'd better not go down that road.

What happened next really reinforced my guilt, as I heard my son utter something unexpected as he wistfully shared his hope. "I always wanted to see Saturn and its rings." He turned to Ben and continued, "I think we can only see it in the early morning this time of year. Right?"

"Yes," replied Ben, as he smiled in agreement. "Towards the end of December, in this hemisphere, you can view it about 45 minutes before sunrise, just above the horizon."

I turned to my husband in surprise and whispered, "Wow! I had absolutely no idea that Alex had any interest in Saturn at all." This insight really scared me because our son obviously knew quite a lot about Saturn and he must have mentioned it several times, but I just wasn't paying attention.

Right before bedtime, Ben and Sara announced, "Don't forget, tomorrow is the Christmas Eve treasure hunt."

Kevin and Mia joined in exuberant yells of glee as they practically jumped around for joy.

"That will give them something to think about," laughed Sara. "We each plan a surprise. It starts with the Christmas Eve treasure hunt, which is actually more like a scavenger hunt. We have to follow the clues to find something to either share with that person or something special showing we care for or love that person. Sometimes the clues are puzzles or games. Often it includes finding a clue in a book. We most often pick our Tom Sawyer novel and they have to locate a particular passage on a specific page which will indicate the next step in the journey."

Ben smiled as he added, "Yes, the journey is just as important as the gift or prize at the end. Our games have gotten more complicated as the kids got older, but believe me, they've come up with some real challenging ones for us too."

Kevin piped up with, "Yeah, like our chess games."

"Oh, come on, now. No fair bringing that up," laughed his dad.

"Tell us. Please?" Alex joined in with delight. "This sounds good. I love chess!"

"Okay, I'll tell you," Kevin volunteered with excitement.

"Hey, he's only going to tell his version. He out and out tricked me," his dad defended himself.

Kevin was not deterred as he eagerly started, "Well, a couple of years ago, the clues went from checkers to chess. Now we'd have to play a game of chess before we could proceed to the next step. The year Dad was trying to teach me how to play, I wasn't very good, of course. However, I really liked the game and I wanted to surprise him the following year at Christmas."

"I didn't tell Mom or Dad that I joined the Chess Club at school and played as often as possible. The teacher would give us pointers and strategy coaching. By the time our Christmas break came around, everyone in our club was fairly skilled at competing."

"Hey, that was no fair, keeping that from me. I wasn't prepared," joked his dad proudly.

Kevin smiled as he continued. "So, Christmas Eve came, and sure enough, one of the clues was: 'Play a game of chess and you will get your next clue.' Well, I beat my dad! He just couldn't believe it. He looked at the chessboard, and then he just looked at me. He finally shook his head in confusion."

We were all laughing and joking with Ben, and it was just plain fun. With an odd sense of regret, I tried to remember when I'd shared such a warm delightful evening with my husband and children. Nothing similar came to mind.

The kids were all up early the next morning, secretly plotting and trying to figure out what was in store for them. The laughter in the tower echoed through the lighthouse. Their part was to do extraordinary deeds to make Christmas special.

Kevin told Alex, "I've always dreamed of actually decorating the outside of the lighthouse with a great light design. It would normally be way too hard for me to do by myself, but if you're game, we can do a spectacular job this year. We can take decorating to a whole new level, with lights all around the railings at the top and everywhere we can reach!"

"You can count on me!" exclaimed Alex. "Where are you going to get all the lights? We'll need a bunch if we plan to do a really great job."

"That's not a problem. We always buy strings of Christmas lights on clearance after the holiday. You won't believe how many we have!"

Meanwhile the girls had discovered their own gift to the family. Sophia had been in a Christmas play on the last day of classes at school which ended with them all singing 'I Heard the Bells on Christmas Day.' Sophia was absently humming the melody of that song as she climbed the steps of the spiral staircase in the lighthouse. Mia knew the song also, and as they began to sing together, the echo of the sweet music filled the tower. That's when they came up with the idea to sing some carols for their Christmas gift to the two families.

"I think we have an old Christmas songbook in the cellar with the other stuff," said Mia.

That's where they met up with the boys.

"Hey, what are doing down here?" asked Mia.

"We're looking for Christmas lights. What are you girls doing?" asked Kevin.

"We want to surprise our moms and dads by singing Christmas carols and I thought I remember a songbook being down here."

"We just heard you singing in the lighthouse. That was amazing," said Alex.

"Hey, I've got an idea!" said Kevin. "We wanted to decorate the lighthouse with all the lights we can find. I know Mom wants to have the lobster bake on the beach tonight for Christmas Eve. Why don't we surprise them with our own Christmas Eve present?"

The kids spent most of their day working on their gift, which was ironic because this essentially put their Christmas Eve treasure hunt on the back burner. However, after lunch, Ben announced, "If you're done eating, look under your chairs and you will find your first two clues taped under two of the seats. Good luck and we'll see you at the finish line."

"Yay, look I have one!" yelled Mia. "It says, 'Let's hope it didn't sink!'"

"Mine says, 'It might be docked,'" called Sophia.

"I'll bet it means your boat. Let's go!" Kevin shouted as he took off toward the water where their sad boat was tied up.

The next few hours were filled with guesses, clues, cookies, hot chocolate, and along the way, games of chess.

One of the last clues was: 'Go to the shed and check the rack.'

"Come on, let's go to the tool shed," Mia yelled in delight, as the kids all took off running.

When they got to the shed, the note on the door said:

'Don't dig and labor in the sand,
Til a metal detector is in your hand!'

"Oh boy!" shouted Kevin as he threw open the doors. Hanging on the rack were two brand new metal detectors with giant red bows.

"Can you believe it?" Kevin asked. "A metal detector is the only thing we asked for."

"Wow, we've got two," exclaimed Mia. "This is the best."

Kevin and Mia put their heads together and agreed to let Alex and Sophia use the new metal detectors while they were visiting. They took the two older ones from the shed and the four kids happily took off to see what they could discover in the sand. After hours of chasing the clues and some great detective work, the successful Christmas Eve treasure hunt came to an end.

My husband took my hand and led me up to the top of a hill to watch the sunset. It was a gorgeous view. The ocean waves, the sea breeze, the sky: it was wonderful. He gently said, "You know, it's been years since I've seen you this happy on Christmas Eve. You seem so relaxed.

In fact, you look like you have enjoyed the last couple of days with the kids and me more than I can ever remember."

I laughed as I admitted, "You know, you're right. I'm not feeling one bit of my usual Christmas pressure. Sara and I have been busy, but none of it makes us feel overwhelmed or stressed out. In fact, we are having a great time."

Joe chuckled as he added, "Do you realize those kids haven't complained about their gadgets or mentioned how bored they were even one time?"

The couple from the lighthouse had set some lobster traps, and the next activity was a delicious Christmas Eve cookout. The kids all helped build the fire and gather and spread the seaweed over the lobsters and corn on the cob. The food was absolutely delicious again.

Just as the sun was sliding out of sight, we noticed the kids were doing a lot of whispering and we knew something was up. A couple of minutes later, Kevin stood and nodded as a signal to the other kids, who joined him. With his eyes beaming, he announced, "To the best parents in the whole wide world: This is our Christmas surprise for you!"

The four children each kissed their moms and dads and waved to them as they headed to the lighthouse. Mia turned backwards after a few steps and called to us, "Please give us five minutes."

We weren't going anywhere, that's for sure!

"We knew they were up to something special this morning. I can't wait to see what they've come up with," I said. I must admit I had a lump in my throat, sensing this love from my children. It was so different from the distant, cut off feelings of the ride in the SUV on Christmas Eve Eve. Could that have possibly have been ... just yesterday?

Moments later, the whole lighthouse burst out with a magnificent display of Christmas lights. The very top along the edges of the cupola roof, as well as both the railings along the widows walk and the gallery walk were strung with endless, bright, glowing lights. The large tree outside the Keeper's Cottage was also decorated with so many lights that it could be seen for miles.

Sara explained, "We don't have a tree inside the house because the huge one outside makes a perfect Christmas tree that we can share with anyone that might be sailing in these waters around this time."

The next thing we heard was totally unexpected. The sweet melodic sound of Sophia and Mia singing, 'I Heard the Bells on Christmas Day' drifted down to us. The echo and the acoustics from inside the lighthouse tower were astonishing. Their voices blended into pure, innocent, clear notes, reminiscent of a children's choir.

The angelic girls sang all four verses, which told the poignant story of what Christmas meant. That simple, yet powerful song was the sweetest carol I'd ever heard. Between the beautiful Christmas lights and the equally beautiful Christmas carols, I'm teary eyed as I wondered if I'd ever have another Christmas this great again.

Christmas morning, right before dawn, we had a surprise for Alex. "Wake up, Alex. Hurry!"

Kevin woke up too and wanted to know what was going on.

"Hurry, both of you. We need to get up to the top of the lighthouse. Kevin, your dad is setting up the telescope on the widows walk outside the lantern room."

"Oh boy!" shouted Alex as he scrambled to find his shoes. "Are you kidding me? Do you think we can see Saturn with its rings?"

"Well, that's the plan. We are having a Christmas breakfast up in the lighthouse watch room, on the floor below the lantern room."

"Wow, this is the best Christmas ever," cried Alex, as the boys raced up the spiral steps of the lighthouse stairway.

Sara and I were setting up the Christmas breakfast when we overheard all the commotion about Saturn and Alex's comment.

She turned to me with tears in her eyes, and said, "Yes, it is the best Christmas ever. Thank you for coming. Your family is amazing!"

I was dumbfounded. "What are you talking about, Sara? We didn't come here, not on purpose. Our boat rental sputtered out and Ben was able to safely get us ashore."

Sara just shook her head. "The only thing I prayed for this Christmas was for our children to be around happiness and feel goodness touch their lives."

"What do you mean?" I asked quietly "Your kids are remarkable."

"My children have seen way too much tragedy in their young lives. I am concerned that they will see life through that prism of grief and mourning. Ben and I chose this life, on purpose, because we love it and it reflects our values for saving lives. I don't want our kids to feel the death and sadness we see, but instead feel the spirit that we can save lives by choosing to be lighthouse keepers."

I was genuinely shocked by this statement. "Well, I can tell you what I see in your whole family. Since we arrived here, I've been touched by your closeness and caring spirit. I've re-thought my entire Christmas attitude and I'm going to change. My kids deserve what your children have."

Christmas that year was life-changing! Joe and I took a very long walk along the shore. We tried to figure out how we could duplicate the time we had just spent together over the last couple of days.

Next, we asked Ben and Sara to join us as we shared our new plans. Together, we created a handwritten contract for Joe and I to buy a scenic 3-acre plot of land, just a short walk from the lighthouse. We were able to build a delightful get-away cottage, which was finished by summer vacation that year. To this day, Ben and Sara and our kids are the best friends we could ever ask for. We now have a wonderful place to visit several times a year.

As we headed back to the boat rental place, we felt like the luckiest family in the world. There was no one around when we tied up their sad little boat, so we left them a heartfelt thank you note. We returned the next weekend and personally delivered their first annual Thank You Gift Basket.

So, let's review:

Did you ever wonder how you would get all your Christmas shopping done in time?

I'm spending every Christmas enjoying my family and friends at our cottage.

How about those decisions regarding what to get each person on your list?

I now spend personal time throughout the whole year, actually listening to those I care about, and my gifts are often things like telescopes, trips to conservatories, books about ship wrecks and sunken treasure, and voice lessons. I also join my family and friends, designing outrageously clever Christmas Eve treasure hunts.

Do you ever question if that person you were trying so hard to please would even remember what you finally gave them?

Never!

Merry Christmas!

What Henrik the Elf Told Santa
Madalin Bickel

"Santa, Santa, I know you're very busy, but Henrik is insisting he talk to you."

It was a dangerous request given that Christmas was just two weeks away and there were mounds of letters not yet read. Han the elf had just hurried into Santa's office. Han hurried everywhere. He thought he was one of Santa's top elves, dressed in traditional green and red, and was always making himself known to Santa.

Saint Nicholas, Kris Kringle, or Santa Claus (whatever you call him) looked up from his desk heavy with unopened envelopes, curled pieces of paper, which were probably lists, and mugs of cold cocoa. "What is it now Han? Does Henrik have another grievance? I told him I had no control over the hours he would need to work this month. Tell him to talk to his shop steward."

"Uh, I don't think that's it, Santa," stammered Han. It was bad timing and he hated being the messenger. He clearly felt like he was inside an old typewriter and being punched by little metal hammers.

"I really don't have time for his complaints. Is Suzy Sharp out there? I need her to organize these letters and lists. I must check on that new line of electronics in building Q. Life was so much simpler before electric toys and now there is this digital stuff. Whatever happened to simple board games and Hula-hoops? Loved those chipmunks! Han, get Suzy."

"Right away, Santa."

"Kris, I've told you, I'm just plain Kris."

"Right." Han scurried out and closed the heavy wooden door only for it to open again for Suzy.

Now, as elves go, Suzy just didn't fit the description. No big ears, floppy shoes, or green tights. She was all about efficiency. Rumor had it she came from some place in Austria, but she was close to normal height, didn't have a Slavic name, and was more efficient like the Japanese. As far as elves go, however, Santa had never recruited any elves from eastern Asia. They were more into Ninja and fairies, but he had an open mind and would love to have a cunning elf from Japan who knew about digital stuff.

Suzy immediately began clearing Santa's desk. She placed the dirty mugs on a tray on a side table, stuffed empty torn envelopes into her apron pockets, and shooed Santa out the door—all in one swift motion. "I'll have these letters organized and ready for you when you return."

Santa sighed, took his red cap from the wall hook, and opened the door. "Thanks Suzy. Oh, and if you have time, could you see what is bothering Henrik?" Out the door he hurried before Suzy could say no.

* * *

Suzy organized the letters by age and type of request and placed a box for each category on Santa's desk. In front of the boxes, she stacked several large yellow legal pads and fresh pens for Santa along with a clean mug all ready for fresh hot cocoa. On a side table, she secretly placed her lap top. Suzy could help Santa organize the requests without him knowing she had gone digital by working with her back to him. She was ready.

The door squeaked open and Suzy looked up. The door was open but no one was there. Then she heard a deep "humph," stood up, and looked over the edge of the desk. It was Henrik. She forgot how short some of these elves were.

"Henrik, Santa is not here. Is there something I can help you with?"

A deep bass voice emitted from the tiny frame. "I've been trying to tell Santa, to warn him."

"Warn him? What do you need to warn him about? He really is busy and I doubt if there is anything he doesn't already know."

"It's this GPS stuff. Kids are asking for it and if we give it to them, well the cat- will-be-out-of-the-bag so to speak."

"What are you talking about? GPS, I know what that is, but are the elves giving them to kids?"

If a short elf could look down on a tall efficient one, Henrik did just that. "The kids are asking for them so we are finding a few to give to only the 'best' kids, but those are the ones who will, you know, let-the-cat-out-of-the-bag."

"Cat, what cat? What have cats got to do with GPS? I mean I know what GPS is, but are we really giving kids their own GPS? Does Santa know?"

"Suzy, do you honestly think Santa knows what a GPS is? He just writes down what the kids want and expects us to fill the orders. You know, we have weathered the coming of electricity (loved those big old trains), televisions and radios, even video games and," he rolled his eyes upward, "computers and cell phones, but this is too much."

"Henrik, how many have been requested?"
"Lots."
"What do you mean by 'lots'?"
"Hundreds. And Suzy, it only takes one."
"What do you mean 'it only takes one'?"
"To LET THE CAT OUT OF THE BAG."
"Henrik, you've lost me. I still don't understand what cats have to do with a GPS."

Henrik gave one of his superior sighs usually saved for the younger elves and quietly said, "If we give a child a GPS, he or she will be able to find us. You know, find the North Pole, Santa's Workshop, the whole enchilada! Then what? No more Christmas surprises and the cat-will-be-out-of-the-bag!"

"Henrik, let me see if I understand this. If we give kids a GPS, they might use it to locate the North Pole and Santa's workshop? Is that what you think might happen?

"Suzy, kids are real smart these days. It wouldn't take them long to figure it out."

"But Henrik, they couldn't get here. I mean a GPS is used for getting from one place to another. It doesn't mean they would come here. Does it?"

"Humph. I've said all I'm going to say. I just think someone needs to let Santa know."

The door opened and Henrik left. Suzy plopped down in Santa's chair, not even thinking about where she was. She didn't know what to do next. Should she tell Santa? Kids couldn't find the North Pole. There was too much snow and it was too cold. Plus, their parents wouldn't let them. Suzy continued to think about it and finally decided it wasn't a problem. The children of the world would not come to the North Pole.

* * *

Santa returned, tired and worried, to a well-organized office. There were far too many traditional toys and not enough tech toys for the requests from children. It was always stressful this time of year, but it seemed to be worse than usual. *Why couldn't kids request bats and balls, and dolls that talk?* The lists were longer, kids seemed to expect more, whether they had behaved well or not, and too many of them no longer believed in Christmas or Santa. *Maybe he was getting too old to do this job. Maybe he should retire.* He picked up a bundle of letters, adjusted his glasses on his nose, and sighed. Where was Suzy?

As if by magic, Suzy came bustling through the door. "Santa, I have a fresh cup of steaming cocoa for you and I'm ready to help organize these last few letters. We'll have these orders ready for the elves to fill in no time."

Suzy set the cup on the desk then sat down at her hidden lap top. "Suzy, do you think I'm getting too old for this job?"

"What? Too old? Don't be ridiculous. You've looked the same for a hundred years. You're not changing. It's the rest of the world that's changing."

"Maybe, but if I can't change with the world or even keep up with the times, what am I to do?"

Suzy went over to Santa and gave him a hug. "Santa, the world will always need to believe in you. The way you care about kids and try so hard to fill their dreams – why it's a big part of the spirit of Christmas."

"Maybe so, but I get the feeling it is all just passing me by and kids don't really care anymore."

"Now, drink your cocoa before it gets cold and I'll begin working on these letters. You'll feel better once we're finished." *How in the world was she going to tell Santa about Henrik's concerns?*

Suzy had taken the last of the lists from Santa to give to the elves when a loud knock buckled the workshop door. "Who in the world is that practically knocking down the door...Suzy, see who that is."

Santa pushed the last of his papers aside ready to do one more factory check when the door opened, crashing against the wall. Suzy

144

jumped back just in time to keep from being a mashed elf. A booming voice filled the room, "Who's in charge here?"

Santa rose from his chair while Suzy straightened her hat. "What is the meaning of this intrusion?" Santa moved from behind his desk while grabbing a large paperweight for defense. He looked the stranger up and down. "Who are you?"

"I am the Representative," responded the voice from a very large man. He was dressed in a heavy trench coat and had a felt hat sitting at an angle nearly covering his left eye. "I have come to speak with you about the problem."

Santa slowly set the paperweight back on his desk. He leaned against the wooden edge of his desk and crossed his arms. "What problem?"

"I understood you had been told. Didn't your security team fill you in? I am here to discuss the matter."

"Mr. Representative, first I have no 'security team.' Second, the only problem we have here is filling the children's orders before Christmas, and third, we do not welcome strangers."

"I see." The stranger turned to Suzy. "Do you mind giving us a few minutes alone?"

"Certainly. Santa?"

"It's okay, Suzy, nothing I can't handle. Take those last lists over to building X and have Henrik begin filling them."

Suzy picked up the lists and left the room, closing the door behind her.

When the door had closed, the visitor asked, "May I sit, Santa?"

"Certainly. Would you like some cocoa? I'm sure we can find a fresh cup somewhere." The man shook his head as Santa moved back behind his desk and sat heavily into his chair. The stranger removed his hat and pulled up an overstuffed armchair.

"Santa, I was under the impression one of your elves had alerted you to our security problem. I am Nero Hampton from ICPA. I've been sent here to assist you with our growing security concern."

Santa removed his glasses and took a few minutes cleaning them. He placed the glasses back on his nose and looked at the man. "Mr. Hampton, I do not know what ICPA is or what in the world it has to do with my operation here at the North Pole. As for my elves, Suzy, my office assistant, keeps me informed of all issues. I'm sure we have no security problem here. Why, it's the North Pole, man. No one ever comes here or for that matter even knows where we are...exactly." Santa's voice dropped off as he looked down at the few lists left on his desk. "My only problem is reading through these last few letters that arrived today."

"I see. You are rather isolated, but I'm afraid the rest of the world is about to arrive at your front door."

Santa looked at Mr. Hampton, "What do you mean?"

"I represent a world-wide security organization known as the International Christmas Protection Agency, ICPA. Our job is to insure the continuation of Christmas traditions including protecting Christmas secrets, such as 'how to bake a plum pudding,' 'where to find Frankincense and Myrrh,' and 'the location of Santa's Workshop.' We learned within the last twenty-four hours that there is a serious threat to the discovery of your location by individuals unknown."

"Why, that sounds impossible. How could mere mortals locate us, and even if they did, how would they get here? We've been at this location for hundreds of years."

"Yes, Santa, I know it seems *impossible*, but times have changed and we now live in a technologically advanced society in which it is difficult to keep secrets. There is this fairly new gizmo called a GPS..."

"Yes, I know about GPS. Rudolph and the other reindeer and I have been using them on Christmas Eve for about two years now. Great little gadget."

"I'm glad you understand. The problem, however, is kids and their parents are now in possession of a variety of GPS instruments. We feel it is just a matter of time before they decipher the longitude and latitude of the North Pole and type it into their units. When they do, well, you can guess what will happen next."

"Longitude and latitude...hmm. I mean we are almost exactly zero and so is the temperature. Surely they would not find their way here...."

"You're right about one thing, you are almost zero. True north is different from your exact location, so that will help some, but not entirely. And, there are people with access to their own airplanes who might find their way here either intentionally or accidentally. Then, your secret is out and many of us at ICPA will lose our jobs."

"I see. So, you think this is a real danger?"

"Yes, and I understand it may be compounded by the fact that kids are asking for and getting their own GPS for Christmas. I don't suppose there is any way you could prevent that, is there?"

Santa looked at Mr. Hampton sadly, "I can't deny children their wishes. I wouldn't be Santa if I did. Surely we can find a way around this problem?"

"Perhaps my organization could break with our secrecy long enough to ask for some technical assistance. In the meantime, can you hold off on giving children their own GPS?"

"Well, Mr. Hampton, Christmas is still two weeks away so I won't be delivering any new units to kids, but you might need to worry about ones they already have."

"Good. If they haven't arrived at the North Pole yet, maybe we have some time. I'll get my staff working on the problem and see if we can get some additional help. You carry on as usual."

The two men rose. Santa reached across and shook Mr. Hampton's hand. "Mr. Hampton, if I may be so bold to ask, how did you find us?"

"Why Santa, I used the GPS on my stealth plane."

"Where did you land?"

"Right outside. My plane is not only difficult to see, it makes no noise." He put on his hat and headed for the door. "We'll be in touch, soon."

When Mr. Hampton had left, Santa dropped into his chair more tired than he ever remembered being. This definitely would be a Christmas to remember.

* * *

The next day, Santa was sitting at his desk finishing a scone and cup of cocoa when a knock sounded on his door. "Come in."

The door opened. A voice boomed, "Santa, I need to speak with you."

Santa looked up. The door was open but no one was there. Then he realized it must be one of the shorter elves. He stood and looked over his desk. "Ah, Henrik, I've been expecting you."

Henrik made one of his throat clearing noises and spoke. "Santa, I have been trying to speak with you for several days. I told Suzy we have a problem..."

Santa interrupted, "I understand, Henrik, you know of the GPS problem and tried to warn me. Is that correct?"

"Humph, yes. So, what are you going to do? Are we going to give kids their own GPS?"

"Henrik, you know I must grant children their Christmas wishes. That's what we do, but I have someone working on the problem. Do you have any suggestions?

"I know we must give the kids what they want, but what if the kids or their parents use the devices to find the North Pole? It will be the end of us, of Christmas."

Henrik's voice remained a deep bass, but for the first-time Santa noticed a real concern in Henrik's tone and was impressed. "Henrik, I appreciate your concern and dedication, but as I said, we are working on the problem. If, however, you or any of the other elves have some ideas, please let Suzy or me know."

"Okay, Santa." Henrik turned to leave, "We just wanted you to know, just in case something bad, you know, happened."

Henrik shuffled out the door and pulled it closed.

* * *

Late that night, without Santa's knowledge, many of the elves and other workers gathered in building Q. It was nearly midnight. They sat around on shipping crates and leaned on half-filled boxes. Henrik climbed up on a stack of boxes and began to talk.

"Folks, we have a big problem here at the North Pole, and Santa needs our help. As many of you know, we have been giving kids their own GPS units for a couple of years now. No one thought about what might happen once kids had all this new technology."

Han spoke up, "What do you mean, Henrik? Aren't the kids just playing with the stuff like they always do?"

"Yes, but these new phones and GPS units can do things that none of us thought to consider. In fact, I'm not sure the kids' parents even thought about what their children might do."

Another elf spoke, "What do you mean *might* do? Aren't they just toys?"

"I'm afraid not. These GPS units can find the North Pole. That is, give away our location to the masses. And, as if that were not bad enough, so can the new phones. We just learned the phones have something called 'apps' which do the same thing as a GPS unit. We are no longer safe from the world finding Santa's Workshop."

Voices rose around the room in surprise and some in anger. "Henrik, are you saying it will be the end of us? Of Christmas?"

"I'm afraid that is a real possibility, so we are here tonight to see if we can help Santa solve the problem."

"Why don't we just stop giving kids electronics for Christmas?" one elf asked.

Another responded, "That would destroy the spirit of Christmas."

Suzy stood up. "Henrik, I have an idea. We have a new elf who arrived from Tokyo last week. She has been observing our work. Friends, this is Sasha Yoyo."

Henrik's eyes brightened as he watched the new elf make her way forward. She was about four feet tall and had the most beautiful almond eyes and ebony hair. When she spoke, it was like a nightingale."

"My dear elf friends. I have just arrived with good news. I have studied the GPS and know how it works. It uses satellites hovering over the earth and sends and receives information from them. There is a satellite near the North Pole."

"What is a satellite?" asked one small voice seated to the back.

"It is a magical ball that floats around the earth. Countries around the world have placed them in orbit to make communication easier for people everywhere, but now the satellites are very close to us and that is the problem."

Suzy spoke, "Sasha, how can we keep the satellite from giving our location to the world?"

"We need to hide Santa's Workshop from the satellite."

Questions of how and when filled the warehouse. Before Sasha could answer or Henrik could quiet the group, a thunderous sound echoed throughout the building. A group of people came striding down the middle of the warehouse with Santa in the lead.

Santa's voice boomed. "What is going on here? Don't you elves have work to do?"

Before the group of dedicated workers could flee, Santa started laughing and turned to the group of people behind him. "My dear friends from ICPA, see what you must compete with? These fine workers may have already solved our problem." Santa laughed and grabbed Mr. Hampton by the shoulder.

"My dear elf friends, I want you to meet Mr. Hampton. He represents an organization who very much wants to protect the location of our workshop, and what we do. He is here to help."

Cheers and laughter bounced around the room as elves slapped each other on the back and hugged in relief.

Mr. Hampton spoke. "I understand you have been discussing our little problem and that one of you has an idea."

Henrik bellowed, "Indeed we do. Meet Santa's newest elf, Sasha. She has a suggestion."

"Sasha," Santa smiled and greeted her. "Please tell us what you think.

"Well, I understand satellites can find us, so we need to find a way to hide so they can't find us."

"Ah, Mr. Hampton. What do you think? Can we hide the North Pole?"

"Indeed, we can. In fact, we have. Just look."

With a rumbling sound the large bay doors of the warehouse opened. The elves, followed by Santa and the men from ICPA, made their way out the door. It was dark as it always is in December, but the light from the warehouse reflected off the snow. There above them, covering all the area of Santa's Workshop, was a large net canopy.

"Camouflage!" yelled the elves as they stared up in wonder at the huge net fluttering in the slight wind.

"Not just camouflage," said Mr. Hampton, "but electronic camouflage. It has a system which will distort signals between us and the satellites."

Santa added, "It will confuse the satellites and make them report that nothing is here. Problem solved."

Cheers erupted in the cold night air. Soon the members of ICPA left in their plane and the elves retired to their little houses. Santa entered his workshop and sat down at his desk. He hadn't told Suzy that her hidden lap top would no longer work, but that was a problem for another day.

There was only one letter left to be answered. He took the letter opener and slit the envelope. A small note fell to his desk. He unfolded the paper and read:

"Santa, could you please send a puppy this year to my house. My grandma is hard of hearing and a puppy would help her so much. I promise to help take care of it. Thank you. Love, Sarah"

Santa said to himself, "I think I could do that, Sarah." He signed the letter and dropped it in the out basket on the desk. Suzy would take care of it tomorrow.

About the Authors

Madalin Bickel writes under the pen name of m. e. jackson. Madalin is an award winning writer from Fredericksburg, Virginia. She is a native West Virginian having moved to Virginia in 2003. She retired in 2012 after teaching for over forty years in both public schools and higher education. Her collection of poems, *Notes From a Failed World*, was released in September 2016. The collection deals with aging and living with an autoimmune disorder. A second collection, *Some Kind of Alternate Universe*, was released November of 2016. The second collection reflects her Appalachian heritage.

  Madalin earned both her BA and MA from Marshall University. She is a member of Riverside Writers, Lake Authors writers group, the Virginia Writers Club, Poetry Society of Virginia, West Virginia Writers, and the Academy of American Poets. She has had poems published in several anthologies by Riverside Writers and in *Scratching against the Fabric*, an anthology published by Bridgewater College, from the 2013 Bridgewater International Poetry Festival.

* * *

Bronwen Chisolm grew up in Central Pennsylvania, the youngest of four sisters by ten years. With such an age gap, she was left to her own imagination much of the time. She became an avid reader at a young age with a love for the classics, Louisa May Alcott, the Bronte sisters, Margaret Mitchell, and many others.

Her love of books and literature could have led her to a career as a librarian. Instead, life and love carried her to Virginia where she took a position as a state employee and began raising her family.

As her children grew and became involved in their own interests, Bronwen returned to her love of the written word. No longer content to simply read, she began writing. Though the first attempts ended up on a shelf for now, she would not be discouraged.

Deciding to set aside her Women's Fiction and Suspense Romance for a time, she finally became a published author with her Pride and Prejudice Variations. Bronwen was thrilled with the acceptance of her first offering, The Ball at Meryton: A Pride and Prejudice Alternative Novella.

She takes great pleasure in searching for potential "plot twists" and finding the way back to a happy ending. Her current work is told entirely from Georgiana Darcy's point of view and has been well received.

Bronwen's love of writing has led her to several writing groups, and she is currently serving as the Vice President of The Riverside Writers. She also heads up the Riverside Young Writers and is on the steering committee for the Lake Authors.

* * *

Mari K. Eder Major General Mari K. Eder, U.S. Army (Retired) served for 36 years in the U.S. Army and has had a distinguished career in public relations and diplomacy. She is the author of *Leading the Narrative: The Case for Strategic Communication,* a respected text now in use by several universities in their mass communications departments.

She is also the author of two books of children's stories, *1001 Places to Pee Before You Die* and *Party Pooper.* These books are based on the adventures of Benson and Maggie, two Miniature Schnauzers with a talent for trouble. Sales of these books benefit animal rescue groups and are available on Amazon.

She is working now on a World War II historical novel, while the first novel in her thriller series is pending publication.

* * *

J. Allen Hill lives in rural Virginia, inspired by the history that surrounds her. She has been writing most of her adult life, first as a school administrator in charge of producing newsletters, enrichment class lessons and the flurry of papers that parents receive daily.

Under contract to the Department of Defense in the Pentagon, she managed a tech support group responsible for the project help desk, application training and testing, all of which required a mountain of written material. She polished her literary skills writing winning speeches as a Toastmaster, her own presentations and tour scripts as a docent at James Madison's Montpelier, and as participating editor of several organizational newsletters, including Fairfax County Parks.

Retirement provides the time to write for pleasure, drawing on a background of many classes, extensive reading, theater, a love of history and the English language. She has published two novels and a book of short stories: *The Secret Diary of Ewan Macrae, The Cause. The Odyssey of Daniel Grant, A Walk in the Park and Other Journeys.*

* * *

Chuck Hillig was born in Chicago and holds two Masters degrees. He has enjoyed successful careers as a commissioned officer in the U.S. Navy, a social worker in New York City, a college instructor at a state university in Pennsylvania, and as a juvenile probation officer for the County of Los Angeles. Before retiring to Virginia in 2006, Chuck worked as a state-licensed psychotherapist in California for almost three decades. Over the years, he has written five easy-to-understand books (published in seven languages) that combine the practicality of western psychology with the wisdom of eastern philosophy. *That's Not My Job!* is one of Chuck's very few works of fiction. His website is www.chuckhillig.com

* * *

Allita Irby was born in Germany to an U. S. Army family and grew up between Frankfurt, Germany and Lawton, Oklahoma. She graduated from Bowie State University with a Bachelor of Arts in Sociology and a Masters of Administrative Science from John Hopkins. She retired from Verizon after 20+ years in Maryland and Washington D.C, and then spent ten years with the Maryland National Capitol Park and Planning Commission Dept. of Parks & Recreation in Prince George's County MD.

Allita spends her time between Bowie, MD and Locust Grove, VA pursuing her artistic interests, writing and reading. A book lover and avid reader all her life, Allita belongs to several book clubs and writing groups. She is the coauthor of the novel, **Fourth Sunday, the**

Journey of a Book Club, published in 2011 by Simon & Schuster under the pen name B. W. Read. See www.bwread.com.

Professional memberships and volunteer services include: Riverside Writers chapter of the Virginia Writers Club and Lake Authors Club, past board member of The Zora Neale Hurston/Richard Wright Foundation in Washington, DC.
Email: airby9@gmail.com, Twitter:@airby9

* * *

Elaine Lewis: Educated at Brooklyn College and University of Mary Washington, Elaine has been a resident of LOW for 28 years where she continues to pursue long-term interests in art, music, poetry, and writing. She has written books of poetry and a children's early reader, ***Grammy and the Night Visitor***.

A booklet of poetry is included with her CD of original music for piano. She is a member of Riverside Writers and Lake Authors, founder of LOW Art for Fun, and has shared her works performing for various groups.

* * *

Julie Phend loves everything about books: reading, writing, discussing, speaking and teaching about them. An educator for many years, Julie holds a BA in English and Theater from Valparaiso University and an MS in education from the University of Wisconsin.

Her first book, **D-Day and Beyond: a True Story of Escape and POW Survival**, was co-authored with Stanley Edwards, a WWII veteran she met when he spoke to her students about his experiences during the war. Since then, she has completed a novel of historical intrigue during the American Revolution titled **Sculptor and Spy**, and is currently working on a middle grade novel. Having spent so much time with longer works, Julie found it fun to write the two short pieces that appear in this anthology.

Julie lives in Lake of the Woods with her husband, Jack. She is an active member of the Lake Authors Club, Riverside Writers of Fredericksburg, and the Society of Children's Book Writers and Illustrators. Website: www.juliephend.com, julie.phend@gmail.com.

* * *

C.A. Rowland is an award-winning writer who has published short stories and non-fiction articles. She is currently finishing her first amateur sleuth paranormal mystery, set in Savannah, Georgia. In addition, she is one of the authors on the Mostly Mystery blog which provides resources, interviews and personal experiences of writers.

C.A. is a member of Lake Authors, Sisters-in- Crime Central Virginia, the Virginia Writer's Club and Riverside Writers.

* * *

Suzi Weinert: As a military wife for 21 years, Suzi Weinert moved often, shopping for practical items at military thrift shops and later for unique treasures at garage and estate sales. When her husband retired, she and her family lived for 25 years in McLean, Virginia, the setting for her garage sale mystery novels. Now with her children grown and flown, she and her husband live in Ashburn, Virginia.

Suzi's three published mystery thrillers include **Garage Sale Stalker, Garage Sale Diamonds** and **Garage Sale Riddle**. She's working on her fourth book, **Girl at the Garage Sale**.

"Every sale reflects a story," she says, and apparently Hallmark agrees. Based on Suzi's work, their **Garage Sale Mystery Series** starring Lori Loughlin has aired 7 original TV movies on their Hallmark Movie & Mystery Channel, with more on the way.

Suzi is a member of Mystery Writers of America and Sisters in Crime. Her website is www.SuziWeinert.com

* * *

W. Rosser Wilson is a retired surgeon who has turned to fiction writing. During his career as a university teaching surgeon, Wilson co-authored two books and published numerous scientific papers. However, upon retirement, his writing interest turned to the challenge of fiction, "a discipline that requires a totally different form of English syntax, a wonderful challenge, and a lot of imagination." Wilson has published two novels, **Otto Danish-American**, and **Insanity by Murder, a Cidee Washington Mystery**, which was a finalist for Outskirts Press 2016 Best Book of the Year award. He currently lives in Virginia with his wife and dog.

* * *

jd young is an author and editor. She has authored two creative non-fiction books, **Scarlett's Letters** and **The Butter Pecan Diaries**, a political thriller, **The Woman on Pritchard Street**, and a book of horror short stories, **Dancing With Demons and Other Bedtime Stories**. A member of the American Copy Editors Society she has edited six books for publication.

She is finishing another dark mystery, **Evangeline de Mercy Sanctuary** and is writing a book on New York cops in the South Bronx. Originally hailing from that area, she is comfortable in the genre.

A member of several writing groups in Virginia, she has taught writing classes for the Windmore Foundation for the Arts in Culpeper, Virginia and a member of *Sisters in Crime.*

A displaced Bronx native, she enjoys semi-retirement with her husband in a bucolic section of Virginia and loves to visit her daughter in Brooklyn. Website: www.jdyoungauthor.com

* * *

Carolyn Zacheis enjoys writing fiction. One of her most beloved subjects is lighthouses, a frequent theme of her fiction, including her anthology piece, *Our Three Hour Tour, Christmas Surprise.* She is a current member of the United States Lighthouse Society and has seen numerous lighthouses on her travels to Asia, Europe, The Caribbean, Bermuda, Tahiti and America, including Alaska and Hawaii. Her writing also reflects her knowledge of the customs of countries where she has visited.

Carolyn Zacheis has recently completed James Patterson's Writing Master Class to enhance her writing skills.

Carolyn's beliefs in the Golden Rule and acts of kindness interweave through her writing. These values were evident during the time she served as President of the Kiwanis, board member of a homeless shelter and the Educational Coordinator at the Literacy Council.

Made in the USA
Middletown, DE
18 September 2017